Learning to cook...

I backed out of the kitchen and untied Mindy Blue, trying not to move too fast, in case Zeuxippe Smith could see how scared I really was ... Then Mindy and I turned and headed for home. Fast.

Meat ... The witch's voice rang in my ears. *Soon we add the meat!*

I actually felt those scaly fingers on my bare arm. And shivered ...

Don't miss Natalie and Denny
in the first two Magical Mysteries

MY AUNT, THE MONSTER
and

WHITE MAGIC

"A delightful new series, with a pair of charming but flawed kids who act like real siblings, save that they keep stumbling into genuine magic ... Seasoned with a hint of deeper mysticism, this is fine and lively writing that will appeal to any kid with a taste for the fantastic ... I can't wait to see what else Mary Stanton has up her enchanted sleeve."
—Bruce Coville, author of *My Teacher's an Alien*

"Mary Stanton's Magical Mysteries are the stories that every child dreams of but rarely finds. Natalie and Denny have the style, pace and plots to push *Goosebumps* to the back of the rack."
—Charles Sheffield, creator of *Jupiter Line*
Young Adult Science Fiction Novels

"The Magical Mysteries are funny, exciting adventures. Magic, science, horses, kids, other worlds—what more could anyone want, at any age?" —Nancy Kress, author of *Oaths and Miracles*

Books in the Magical Mystery Series

MY AUNT, THE MONSTER
WHITE MAGIC
NEXT DOOR WITCH

NEXT DOOR
Witch

A Magical Mystery

* ★ * ★ * ★ * ★ *

Mary Stanton

BERKLEY BOOKS, NEW YORK

NEXT DOOR WITCH

A Berkley Book / published by arrangement with
the author

PRINTING HISTORY
Berkley edition / July 1997

The Putnam Berkley World Wide Web site address is
http://www.berkley.com

ISBN: 0-425-15905-1

BERKLEY®
Berkley Books are published by The Berkley Publishing Group,
200 Madison Avenue, New York, New York 10016.
BERKLEY and the "B" design
are trademarks belonging to Berkley Publishing Corporation.

PRINTED IN THE UNITED STATES OF AMERICA

10 9 8 7 6 5 4 3 2 1

For Julie, who knows
Natalie well

ACKNOWLEDGMENTS

My thanks to John Blitz, Ph.D., for help with the spell and to my friend Deborah Howie, for two significant questions.

NEXT DOOR Witch

CHAPTER

ONE

THE HORSE BARN WAS PROBABLY THE WORST PLACE I've ever seen in my life. Well, it wasn't exactly a horse barn. Not a proper barn with stalls and clean sawdust on the stall floors and nice green hay in the corners. It was a shed where this poor horse lived.

It was terrible.

This was late June, and it was *hot*. The shed had a tin roof that meant it was hotter inside than outside. The paddock was piled with manure that had been there for years, probably. A zillion flies buzzed all over me.

A bucket in the corner of the paddock was filled with slimy scum, which was all the poor thing had to drink. All I could see of the horse who lived there was a thin, scraggy tail.

I was so mad I couldn't get any words out. Finally,

my breath got unstuck, and I whistled and called, "C'mon, boy," which practically any horse will pay attention to.

An old, old horse stumbled out of the hot shed into the paddock. His coat—what you could see of it through the mud and the burrs—had been a beautiful silvery color about a million years ago. Now it was patchy and covered with manure. His head hung down to his knees and his eyes were cloudy.

"Jeez," said my little brother Denny.

The dumbest thing was, this mess was surrounded by a brand-new chain-link fence. I mean, why spend piles of money on a chain-link fence to keep in a horse that could hardly even walk?

Nope. The dumbest thing wasn't that fence. The dumbest thing was that my little brother Denny and I were standing looking at this and not doing a single thing about it.

"C'mon, Denny."

Denny's seven years old. I half expected him to do his usual bratty stuff and refuse to do what I said just because it was me saying it. I mean, even a seven-year-old should know that a fourteen-year-old like me has enough smarts to figure out the world. Not smarty-pants Denny. He's got a definite stubborn streak under his spiky red hair.

He didn't give me any lip this time, though. The situation was way too serious.

So we climbed the fence, which wasn't all that easy. My hair got tangled up in the wire. I practically wrecked my new pair of Gap jeans. The lace collar ripped on my favorite pink T-shirt. But we did it.

This horse was glad to see us. I went over and petted it, stroking its withers in a soothing kind of way. A thin ridge of scar tissue was on each shoulder under the scaly dirt. Scars like this sometimes come from saddle sores and not keeping your horse clean like you should.

This dirty, silvery horse looked at me and whinnied. His whinny didn't sound as pathetic as he looked. It was a clear strong sound, like a trumpet. I figured a horse that could sound like that might not be so bad off after all.

"That's Old Peg there, that is."

I jumped about a foot. A woman stood on the other side of the fence looking in. She was dressed all in black. Black turtleneck. Black droopy skirt that went to the ground and covered her shoes. Her hair was black, too. It was pulled back in a tight knot that stretched the skin of her face. She was short and round and had the kind of face that should be smiley, but isn't.

For some reason, she scared me. And not just because Denny and I were inside her fence when we shouldn't have been. For one thing, she was smooth all over, like a big plastic doll. And she didn't have any bends in her clothes. I mean, a person just naturally has bends in their clothes from knees and elbows and like that. Her face didn't have any bends or wrinkles either. When she smiled it was just her lipsticked mouth changing shape.

I poked Denny not to stare. Mom says there's all kinds of room for all kinds of people on this planet, but this person wouldn't have fit in anywhere I'd ever seen. Anyhow, I said, "Sorry, ma'am. We didn't mean to break in or anything."

She just grinned that weird grin. She rubbed her hands together and said, "This is so nice! You've come about the job, haven't you? I just know you nice strong children have come to help me with poor Old Peg."

I didn't much like the way she called us nice strong children, but a lot of adults are like, clueless, so I said pretty politely, "That's right, ma'am. I'm Natalie Ross and this is my brother Denny. Like I said, we're sorry about climbing over your fence."

"Call me Zoo-zip-ee," she said, totally ignoring this apology. Then, just like this Mr. Rogers on Denny's old TV program: "Can you say Zoo-zip-ee? It's spelled Z-E-U-X-I-P-P-E."

"Yes, ma'am."

"That's Greek, you know, for horse tamer. Not that dear Old Peg needs any taming." A mean little light flashed in her eyes. I blinked. I was getting confused. Her words were okay, but the way she said them wasn't. And that flash in her eyes—was it hate? Then she said in a voice like she'd just swallowed a big greasy doughnut, "At least, he doesn't need taming anymore."

"Peg's a girl's name," said Denny. "How come a horse that's a him has a girl's name?"

I didn't pay any attention this. Zeuxippe Smith didn't either.

Actually, I did know that Zeuxippe was a Greek word for horse tamer. I even knew how to pronounce it. Dad had made me look it up in the dictionary last night when I told him I wanted to get a job. I'd shown him the card I'd brought back from the job board in the supermarket.

I'd better explain about this job stuff. Mom, Dad, Denny, and me were spending summer vacation in a rented house near my uncle Bart's horse farm in up-state New York. During the year we all live in Manhattan, where Mom and Dad have an advertising agency. Usually, they send Denny and me to spend summers at Uncle Bart's by ourselves. Dad says Manhattan's no place for a kid in summertime. This year Mom and Dad came with us. So this year was different.

As a matter of fact, this year a *lot* of things were different. For one thing, I had to get a job. Well, I didn't *have* to, exactly. I wanted to earn twenty-five dollars and fast. Uncle Bart had just hired a cool new riding instructor. This instructor was giving a week-long clinic, starting tomorrow. For two hours every afternoon for a week, I would learn to jump fences on my mare, Mindy Blue. Dad'd said he'd pay for most of the clinic if I paid for a quarter of it. So I had to earn twenty-five dollars pretty fast. The clinic was expensive.

Now, there were a lot of other things that made this summer different from other summers. But I'll get to that. Anyhow, the only jobs around for kids like me were part-time things, like this barn-cleaning job Zeuxippe Smith had advertised for.

I'd found the ad for the job yesterday, stuck on the bulletin board at the Safeway supermarket.

STABLE HAND WANTED
PEGASUS FARMS
ZEUXIPPE SMITH, OWNER
ONE CORY CORNERS ROAD

It'd been a cool sort of card, with a flying horse printed in the corner. I showed it to Dad, who checked this Zeuxippe Smith out with Uncle Bart. Uncle Bart said she was new in town. Hadn't been there for very long. People thought she was a widow and she kept to herself.

Working for a quiet widow was just fine with Dad, so he said we could go to her farm for a job interview.

Cory Corners Road was practically next door to our rented house, so after breakfast, I fixed Denny and me a couple of tuna-fish sandwiches in case we got hungry. Then we'd biked to Cory Corners Road for this job interview. It was only about three miles from our house, but it was all uphill. I'd been all sweaty when we'd gotten there, so we'd stopped at the beginning of the driveway to cool off. First impressions are very important when you do a job interview and I wanted to get the job. This was why I was wearing my pink T-shirt with the lace collar. So, I had been combing my hair and brushing off my Gap jeans and not paying too much attention when Denny said, "This is it?"

I had looked around and saw right away what he meant. There was an ugly sign stuck in the ground that said PEGASUS FARMS, so I knew we were in the right place. The flying-horse picture was peeling off it and the Pegasus Farms part was written all scraggly with a Magic Marker. I looked around some more. The farm itself was a big mess. The fences were saggy and the pastures were filled with sticker bushes and dry brown grass.

I had stopped worrying about being sweaty and we walked our bikes up the long gravel driveway. I kept my eyes open for horses, but we didn't see any at all, just a lot of rusted junk and old tires.

I was just thinking that maybe Denny and I should go home, since Dad would have a hissy fit once he checked this place out, when we saw the shed and this poor neglected horse. Denny and I ran right over to help it.

So here we were with this Zeuxippe Smith standing outside the fence, looking in at us.

"You can see things need a bit of tidying up," Zeuxippe Smith said.

A *bit*?

"I'm just not able to keep up with the work here." Her fat fingers fluttered at her chest. They were covered with jewels. Big rubylike stones and a couple of rings that I bet were diamond. "My heart . . . the heat . . . it's too much." Her little black eyes darted sideways. "So. Can you fine strong children clean this up? I'm a poor woman, you know. But if you could help me—and of course, poor Old Peg, here— why, I could probably find a few hard-earned dollars to pay you both."

Denny looked happy at that, the little money-grubber. Me, I was scared for this poor horse. And I wasn't sure what Dad was going to say. This place was . . . well, *creepy*. You could feel it.

A skinny orange cat crept along the inside of the fence. It jumped up on one of the posts and sat looking at Denny and me. Its eyes were green. Sea green. It squeezed them shut and open again. Its fur was a marmalade gold. Like the silvery horse, it was thin and matted with mud. Denny walked over and petted it. Its purr was like an engine with no muffler.

"Well?" said Zeuxippe Smith, a hard note in her voice.

"I really better check with my mom and dad, Mrs. Smith," I said.

Old Peg raised his head and looked at me. My face got hot. I was sure I was going to start sniveling. Those eyes were sad eyes.

"I have hardly any money," said Zeuxippe Smith, "but I do need the help." I looked at her hands, which were fat like sausages. She had gold bracelets on her arms and then there were those rings on her fingers. They looked real, but you never can tell. Even fake jewelry costs money, and of course there was this brand-new fence. That cost a bucket, you can bet. Whatever money she had, she sure wasn't spending it on this horse.

My mom didn't raise any numbskulls. I figured it this way: Denny and I would clean up this poor old horse and this disgusting manure and Zeuxippe Smith wouldn't pay us one thin dime. As soon as I thought this, the cat began to meow in this loud scared way. I ran my hand over Old Peg's withers again and felt the scars. I waited until my throat loosened up and said, "Okay. We'll take the job."

Denny muttered, "Gross."

The cat started to purr again.

There was this guy who'd painted our apartment in Manhattan last year. I remembered Dad had paid him for the paint before he started to work. "We'd be happy to work for you, Mrs. Smith. But Denny and I will have some—some expenses, of course. Could you pay us half now and half when we've finished? Say, maybe twelve dollars and fifty cents?"

Zeuxippe Smith smiled in a way that made me shiver. "Now? When I'm not sure about your qualifications? How do I know you can do the job? You clean up this pen and I'll inspect it. You come and get me when you're finished. Then we'll discuss your pay."

Like I said, my mom didn't raise any bozos. A person mean enough to starve this horse wasn't about to pay us to clean it up and feed it. I had about three bucks on me from my allowance. I was going to pay Denny part of it and promise to pay him all summer for helping me with my new job. But I could kiss that three bucks good-bye, I guess. I figured Denny and I could buy three bucks' worth of oats from the Agway and borrow hay from Uncle Bart. If we didn't help Peg—who would?

"Fine, ma'am," I said. "We'll come up to the house when we're through."

She nodded toward a run-down old house in the middle of some scruffy trees. "It's up that way. I'll be waiting. And if you're very very good, perhaps some cookies?"

"Thanks, ma'am." I wasn't about to take cookies from this person, even if they were double chocolate chunk. I waited until Zeuxippe Smith rolled off toward her falling-down house. Then I rubbed Old Peg's nose. "It's all right, boy. We'll get you some fresh water and some good hay and then we'll get you cleaned up. You're going to feel great."

Denny and I poked around in the shed. In the back of it, outside the chain-link fence, we found this big stack of clean hay and a new garbage can filled with oats! I got even more disgusted than I was. Poor Old Peg could probably smell this good food and here he couldn't reach it. We hauled two thick flakes of hay into the paddock and Old Peg tore into it like he hadn't had a meal for weeks. The skinny cat was pretty hungry, too, I guess, because it wound around our legs meowing. Denny ended up giving it his tuna-fish sandwich. After we cleaned out that mucky bucket and got fresh water in it, Denny and I shared my sandwich. Hauling giant bales of hay around is hungry work.

Then Denny wanted to give Old Peg a huge pile of oats. I stopped him from that. You can't give a horse that hasn't had any food too much of it too fast. It'll get sick with the colic. Horse stomachs are funny that way.

"Peg's hungry," said Denny, and that good old horse nodded like he could understand what we were saying.

"Sorry, Denny. We can't do it." Denny's lower lip stuck out in a way that would mean trouble, if it wasn't me that he was doing it to. Denny can get around you if you don't know him very well. He looks so adorable some people end up doing what he wants even when it's perfectly ridiculous. I mean, that sticking-up red hair and those freckles are—what's the word? Deceptive, that's it. Denny's cute-kid looks were deceptive.

"I know Peg's hungry. But if you give him too much grain, he'll bloat up and die." Which isn't strictly true, but the bloat-up-and-die part shut Denny up at least. You can't give a horse too much of anything all at once. They just eat and eat until they get the colic, and then you're in trouble and so is the horse. "We'll give him a small scoop," I said. "Then when we come back tomorrow, we'll give him a little bigger scoop."

So we gave Old Peg a small scoop of oats and he ate that so fast I had to grab Denny to keep him from giving the horse more.

Once Old Peg got some food down him, I figured we should clean him up a little. Flies were stuck in the manure on his sides and stomach. I looked and looked, but I couldn't find one brush or currycomb in the whole place, which figures. I mean, how can a person keep a horse and not brush it and comb it every day? I combed out Old Peg's mane and tail with my fingers, then used the tail of my T-shirt to wash off some of the manure crusted on his coat. That didn't work very well, but it helped some. Didn't help my new T-shirt much, though.

Then Denny and I pitched manure and raked straw out of that paddock until I thought I'd fall over dead. The cat and the horse watched us for a while. Then they both fell asleep in the sun. By the time my watch said five o'clock, we'd made a pretty good dent in the mess, but we'd have to come back the next day to finish.

"We've got to be *home* by five o'clock," I reminded Denny. "We're already late. Refill the water bucket. Give the last of my sandwich to the cat. I'll go tell *her* we're through for the day."

"Get our money," said Denny.

"I'll try."

I left Denny petting the barn cat and went up to Zeuxippe Smith's house. The house had a pointy peaked roof. The front porch had most of the boards missing. The back porch wasn't much better. It was stacked with junk: rusty bedsprings, old buckets, dirty rags, and piles of moldy newspapers. I stepped over this stuff and looked in the back window.

Zeuxippe Smith kept her kitchen clean as clean, which made me mad all over again. Anybody that can keep a kitchen clean can keep a horse clean, too. Plus, a lot of the appliances in that kitchen were shiny and new. It's one thing if a person is too sick or too poor to take care of animals. It's another when they are just bone lazy. This horrible person could have brought that nice hay around for Peg to eat any-time she wanted to. And fresh water was practically free. All she'd had to do was dump the bucket and fill it a couple of times a day.

The more I peered in the window, the more Zeu-xippe Smith's kitchen gave me the same feeling that she did herself. Like, the kitchen *should* have been normal but wasn't. There was a stove and a fridge and a sink and all that stuff. But the walls didn't have anything on them but racks and racks and

racks of green glass bottles filled with weeds. Herbs,
I guess. There was a square pot on the stove. Who's
ever seen a square pot? Steam came from it. There
was a smell in the air like the rotten egg in a carton
Mom bought by mistake once.

There was no sign of Zeuxippe Smith, but I
knocked at the back door anyhow. The door opened
all of a sudden. I gasped in surprise. Zeuxippe Smith
stood there, like she'd come out of nowhere. She
stretched her mouth in that smile that made no
wrinkles in her cheeks.

"Well!" She was trying to make it nice, but her
voice was cold. Like icicles.

"We're not quite finished, ma'am. We have to get
home to dinner. We can come back tomorrow. But if
we could get paid for the work we've done so far?
Would you like to come and check it out?"

Her mouth snapped shut. "I'm too worn-out to go
hiking out to that pen every minute. And I'm certainly not going to pay you for a job half-done. You
two finish up tomorrow and then I'll be happy to pay
you. Not much, I'm afraid." She patted her chest. The
jewels on her fingers flashed. "This poor old widow
woman doesn't have much."

Denny would go hyperspazz if he didn't get at least
a dollar for all that work. "It won't take too long to
check on what we've done, Mrs. Smith. If—"

All of a sudden Denny was at my back. He pushed
me into the kitchen. Inside, the smell from the boiling pot on the stove was worse than twenty tons of
manure. I gave him my best glare.

Denny ignored me, naturally, and stomped right up to her and said, "How much money do we get?"

I couldn't believe my little brother could be such a bozo. I mean, standing in this woman's kitchen demanding to get paid like he'd lost every single manner he'd ever had. And he sure hadn't many manners to begin with.

"Denny!" I said in this I-really-mean-it whisper.

Her little black eyes glittered. They reminded me of something slimy. "I told your sister I'm not paying you for a job half-done. I am a poor old woman with little of value to offer. You come back tomorrow and we'll see."

"You've got valuable stuff," said Denny. "You've got this." He jumped past her and snatched something from the shelf of green jars.

"Denny!" I shouted. Swiping stuff was too much, even if this person *had* practically starved her horse to death. I grabbed his arm and pried his fingers back from whatever it was.

It was a paperweight. A beautiful crystal paperweight. There was a gold horse floating in the middle. The horse had diamond wings that sparkled. Its eyes glowed with rubies.

"You put that down!" Her voice was terrible. Huge. It grew and grew in the kitchen like a tornado about to hit.

I grabbed that paperweight out of Denny's hand so fast I didn't have time to breathe. I muttered about Denny not understanding about the pay. She turned to me, black eyes glittering in that half-familiar way.

Like a snake, I thought suddenly. Like a giant snake.

This time I was sure I saw that red flash of hate. The same look that had been her eyes when she talked about taming Old Peg. She leaned toward me. Her breath hissed past my ear.

"If he ever touches that again, I'll turn him into a *pig*!"

Her breath was awful, most likely from eating that mess of gunk on the stove. Her eyes locked into mine. I wanted to run like any cowardly jerk, but I stared right back. For a minute it was like some stupid staring contest fifth graders do.

"Well?" she said. "You come back tomorrow. We'll talk about your pay then."

I wanted to come back to this creepy place like I wanted a faceful of zits. But I thought about Old Peg. I couldn't abandon that horse. What I could do maybe was get Dad to call the sheriff. This was animal abuse if anything was. The horse *and* that poor cat. "We'll be in touch," I said, just like Mom on the phone with one of her advertising clients. "Come on, Denny." I backed to the door, pulling Denny along with me. We beat feet out of there and ran for our bikes. I hollered at Denny to move it. We raced along the gravel driveway for what seemed like miles until we came to Cory Corners Road. I kept looking back in case she was rolling after us, but nope, she must have stayed right in her kitchen. I stopped at the road and shouted at Denny to watch for cars. He stuck out his tongue, made a big circle in the middle

of the road on his bike, then pulled a wheelie in front
of me and came to a stop. We were both out of breath.

"Wow," said Denny.

" 'Wow' yourself. Come on. We've got to get home
and talk to Dad. There's no way we can go back there
and rescue that horse ourselves. Dad can call the
sheriff, or something." I started pedaling, but no
Denny. "Denny?" I looked around. Denny was parked
at the end of the drive, ignoring me, like usual.

"Denny!" I pedaled back. "Come *on*! I—" I stopped.
My mouth hung open. I felt like a big fist just up and
slammed me in the stomach.

The gold horse turned slowly in Denny's freckled
hand. The diamond wings glittered. The ruby eyes
sparked like fire.

My little brother had stolen the paperweight.

"Denny!" I kept my voice down, in case Zeuxippe
Smith had already found out the paperweight was
gone and was after us. "You take that *right back*!" I
gritted my teeth. "I'll go with you." I mean, you can't
send your little brother back to mess with a person
who thinks he'd be better off as a pig. Not all by himself.

"Nope!"

"Denny! She'll probably call the police!"

Denny stuck out his tongue. Then he pedaled off
down the road like Superman, faster than a speeding
bullet, the paperweight glittering in his hand.

We were in trouble now!

CHAPTER

two

I PEDALED AFTER DENNY, WONDERING WHAT THE heck was going on. How was I going to get Denny out of this mess without anybody finding out about him? He's not a thief, or anything. At least, not usually. Denny's your normal sort of seven-year-old. Into Spiderman, X-Men, and all that stuff where the good guys are good guys and the bad guys are crooks. What was buzzing around in my brain while I pedaled like a crazy person was the reason this summer was so different. The reason I wanted a job to stay out of everybody's way.

Four months ago, I'd learned that my brother Denny is a magician.

Now, I'd had big-time stress attacks over this magician stuff right after I'd found out about it. For one thing, nobody knows about Denny being a magician but me. Three other people knew about Denny being a magician for a little while, but the magic made them forget they knew, so it's just me and Denny now. Which is this big-time responsibility. The people who *don't* know Denny's a magician include poor old Mom and Dad. If they found out, Mom and Dad would have a major heart attack and want to send Denny off to a child psychologist. This would be totally unnecessary. I mean, I discovered pretty quick that Denny's magic is not that big a deal if you keep an eye on him. Gosh, half the time Denny *forgets* he can do magic. I mean, he's only seven years old. He's got the attention span of these fruit flies I learned about in biology.

And besides, Denny's magic is harmless, most of the time. He can't do anything cool, like make me remember the capitals of European countries in the middle of a geography test. All the magic can do is rearrange the molecules of things. How often can you rearrange the molecules of things without getting into big-time trouble with the rest of the world? Almost never. Trust me on that. And Denny's a bozo a lot of the time, but he'd just as soon not be hassled about his magic any more than I would.

So he keeps the lid on. Usually.

Best of all, Denny can't do much magic at all without me. We need the pearl necklace to do his magic. The pearl necklace is mine. And you can bet Denny doesn't get his sweaty little mitts on that necklace unless it's a crisis. Which means he can stomp off to school without my worrying he's going to turn a bunch of first graders into reptiles.

Life with a little brother who's a magician can be
pretty peaceful as long as nobody notices too much.
Which was the other reason I wanted a job this summer. Nobody notices you if you're out working. This
barn-cleaning job had seemed just about perfect.

Until now.

I pedaled faster. Denny hollered "Yaaaah!", sailed
his bike over the curb, and took off crosslots.

Now that Denny'd snatched that paperweight, I
couldn't tell Dad about the animal abuse. Mrs. Smith
could have Denny arrested anytime for stealing her
paperweight. I couldn't believe Denny was being
such a brat. I couldn't believe that this summer was
going to have more stress.

Stress, stress, stress!

It was all downhill to home. Denny coasted like a
maniac, so he beat me to it. We got there just as Mom
and Dad pulled into the driveway. Mom said it would
be just the four of us for dinner. This was a relief.
Althea Brinker, who takes care of us when Mom and
Dad have to go places on business, was staying at
Uncle Bart's horse farm right near this house we'd
rented. Sometimes she comes for dinner, too, but
Mom said she was helping Bart with evening chores
and wouldn't be over until tomorrow. So that was one
less person to worry about discovering that Denny
had lost his mind and become a thief. It'd be bad
enough if just Mom and Dad found the paperweight
before I figured out what to do.

I hoped like heck that whole idea of saving Old Peg
wasn't, like, out the window.

Between getting the manure washed off us and

helping Mom and Dad get dinner and listening to all the stuff they'd done that day, and being just plain mad, I didn't have two seconds to think about how to save Old Peg. By the time we sat down to eat, I was so mad at Denny for messing up my calling the sheriff, Mrs. Smith could have had him hauled off to the pokey anytime. It would have been fine by me.

One thing I wasn't mad about: it didn't matter one little bit that we weren't going to get paid for cleaning up that crummy shed. What did matter is that Dennis Ross, Junior Crook, had totally bombed my great plan to save Old Peg. I'd been counting on the fact that Mom and Dad would be as mad as I was over the way Old Peg'd been treated. Once the sheriff saw what Zeuxippe Smith had done to that horse, she'd get slapped in the slammer and some good ol' judge would probably sentence her to ninety years of cleaning up horse manure. Which was fine by me. I'd been thinking maybe even the judge would let us take Old Peg to Uncle Bart's, where I could take care of him every day.

Now, if Dad called the sheriff, Mrs. Smith would squawk like anything about her missing paperweight. Everybody would forget about the horse. That same judge would probably sentence Denny to ninety years for swiping stuff. Even though he was just a little kid. And I'd have more stress trying to keep people from finding out about Denny's being a magician. In jail, I believe they watch you all the time with these TV things. It'd be easy for them to find out.

One thing I was sure of, I'd have to come up with

some diversionary tactics. Our soccer coach at school was like a marine or something, and she was big on diversionary tactics. Diversionary tactics are what you do to make somebody think you're doing something else instead of what you're really doing.

I was thinking about Mrs. Smith and how I was pretty sure she wouldn't call the cops on us unless I called the cops on her first, when Dad finally got to how Denny and I'd spent our day. It was in the middle of dinner.

"How'd the job interview go?" Dad asked. He took a big bite of liver. He asked again. I'd been staring at Denny, thinking of the advantages of having him socked away in some jail for a while. It had its attractions. It'd be a great diversionary tactic.

"Fine," I said, giving Denny a big don't-say-a-*word* glare.

"We got the job," Denny blabbed. I kicked him under the table and bugged my eyes out to shut him up.

"You did?" Mom said in this pleased kind of way. "So you'll be able to pay for your part of the jumping clinic. Bart told Dad and me that this new trainer is named Bill Fromm. He's supposed to be a tremendous jumper and teacher."

"Is he from around here?" I asked, to keep this diversionary tactic going.

"Nope," said Dad, "just showed up at Bart's barn to work for room and board a couple of weeks ago. Bart found out he could ride by accident."

"Where is Cory Corners Road, exactly?" said Mom,

getting back to to the point like she does. "Isn't that the address of the Pegasus Farm?"

"Practically next door." Then I thought of another diversionary tactic. I said real fast, "This liver is great, Mom."

"It is?" Mom raised her eyebrows. Big mistake. We only have liver about once a year, which is way too often for me. Mom doesn't forget stuff like that.

"What kind of place is Pegasus Farm?" Dad asked. "Did you like Mrs. Smith?"

About as much as I like liver. "She's a little different," I said, careful like.

Dad got this sharp look he gets when he thinks something's up. "Different how?"

"She's old." This was true. I mean, she wasn't a hundred or anything, but she was at least as old as Mom and Dad. "She said she's very poor." This was what she'd *said*, even though I believed that about as much as I believed Martians lived in Detroit. "So I don't think we'll get much pay. But the horse is cool."

"She'd better pay us," scowled Denny. "You oughta see what we did today. You shoulda seen the mountains of horse poop. You shoulda seen how skinny that poor old horse was."

Denny always puts his Spiderman yo-yo right by his plate when he eats. The Spiderman yo-yo is with him all the time, and it can be a real pain in the neck when he uses it to trip you up or something.

I reached over, grabbed it, and threw it into the mashed potatoes. Coach Noonan would have been proud. Grabbing your little brother's stuff is a *swell* diversionary tactic.

"Hey!" yelled Denny.

"Natalie!" said Mom.

"Oops!" I said. "Slipped out of my hand. You were waving your fork around, Denny, and I thought you were going to drop peas onto it. Didn't want you to goo up the string."

"Honey," said Mom. "You really owe Denny an apology."

I gritted my teeth. Apologizing to Denny always gets to me. "I'm sorry, Dennis." He hates it when I call him Dennis. "Do you want me to clean it off? Or do you want to do it yourself. In the kitchen." That'd get him out of the way for a while.

"I don't want you to *touch* it. Mom, can I be excused?"

"Yes, honey."

Denny grabbed his precious yo-yo, slid off his chair, and stomped off.

Dad looked at me with a little frown. "Natalie. This farm . . ."

"What's 'Pegasus' mean, Dad? Is it a Greek word, like Mrs. Smith's first name?" Now this was a smart diversionary tactic, if I do say so myself. Dad likes nothing better than to educate us.

"Pegasus was a winged horse in Greek mythology, that much I know. I'll look it up after dinner."

Great. Liver, education, and piles of horse manure all in the same day.

I went right to my room after the dishes to try and think my way out of this mess.

I walked into my room and flopped belly-down on the bed, almost forgetting that my cat Bunkie was asleep on my pillow, as usual. I had to give this great big heave halfway down so I didn't squash her. She gave this cranky sort of "meow," jumped off the bed, and walked out of the bedroom. She was mad. I didn't blame her. I was mad, too. This could have been such a totally cool summer and now things were getting complicated. It looked like more stress. Stress, stress, stress! And I thought stuff was going to be so *cool*!

For example: the house that Mom and Dad had rented for the summer was right next to Uncle Bart's horse farm. Back in Manhattan I'd thought this was absolutely the best. I could walk over every morning and see my favorite horse, Mindy Blue. I could talk to Althea anytime I wanted, too. Althea was an okay sort of person even though she was a hotshot science tutor. She had the greatest hair in the entire world, practically. Red and long and curly.

But Althea and Mindy Blue weren't the only reasons I'd thought this summer was gong to be cool. The landlord of this house allowed pets, which was great, since I wouldn't have to leave Bunkie with my best friend, Nan, who only *sort* of liked cats.

I'd even got Denny's being a magician sort of under control. The only thing that could have been more perfect was if Brian Kurlander was around. He's this really good friend of mine. Brian was off on a white-water rafting trip and I wouldn't see him until eighth grade started in September. But he'd given me this perfectly fabulous thing to remember him by:

a charm bracelet with a tiny gold heart on it. The heart was real gold. It was my favorite thing.

Everything had been perfect.

Until now.

I was lying on my back resting from almost squashing my cat when Dad knocked on my door. He had a book in his hand. He came in and sat on the edge of the bed with a happy look on his face. Parents are always happy when you're getting an education.

"I think you're going to find this *very* interesting, Natalie." Dad read from the book. " 'Pegasus is the only winged horse known to Greek mythology. Where he stamped his feet, a river sprang and from the river flowed all the poetry in the world.' "

Good grief.

" 'Pegasus sprang fully formed from the chest of Athena'—that's the goddess of wisdom, Natalie— 'and the only person who could ride Pegasus was Belly-fron. Belly-fron was a handsome youth.' As handsome as say, Brian Kurlander."

I wasn't all that sure that Dad was *reading* that part. His eyes crinkled. I think he was making it up.

" 'And one beautiful spring morning, Belly-fron flew Pegasus straight to Mount Olympus. The mountain of the gods.' "

Now that sounded pretty awesome.

" 'No mortals were allowed to beard the mountain—' "

"Put hair on the mountain?"

"Used that way, 'beard' means to approach. It's an ar-kay-ik usage, Natalie. Used in olden times." He grinned. Dad's got a pretty good grin, especially when he's teaching you something. "Arkayik is spelled A-R-C-H-A-I-C. Archaic. Anyway, the gods became angry. Furious with Belly-fron."

Sort of like me with Denny. I could sympathize with those bearded gods.

" 'Pegasus himself was doomed to act as a pack animal and carry lightning bolts for Zeus.' "

"They punished the *horse*?"

Dad looked over his reading glasses at me. "You don't think it's more terrible that they punished the person?"

Heck, no. "Well, sure, Dad," I said, mainly because it looked like a lecture might be coming on. "That poor thing! And poor Belly-fron, too."

"It's B-E-L-L-E-R-O-P-H-O-N, Nat. Bellerophon. Look, I'll show you."

I was saved from more education by Denny, of all human beings. He walked smack into my room without knocking like he always does, and I said, "Get out" automatically before I remembered that I had to get that darn paperweight away from him and back to Mrs. Smith before something awful happened.

"Denny, my man," said Dad.

Denny has Spiderman everything. Spiderman hat, Spiderman lunch box. Even Spiderman pajamas, which he was wearing now. I just knew he had that dumb Spiderman yo-yo on him, too. He'd just had his bath and his hair was plastered down over his ears. This gave me an idea.

"Your hair's wet, Denny. Let me get my blow-dryer."

Denny screeched, "No!"—which is guaranteed to get Dad stern.

"Nat's right, Denny. It'll take just a few minutes. And you shouldn't go to bed with wet hair."

"I *hate* the blow-dryer!"

Now who hates a blow-dryer, for Pete's sake? I would just have to "beard" Denny and make him do it. "Let me take care of it, Dad."

Dad gave me this grateful look. "Thanks, Natalie. Mom and I will be in to tuck him up in a bit." He gave Denny another stern look. "You obey your sister, young man."

Ha! Served the little bozo right. I tried not to act superior, at least not until Dad was out of the room. As soon as my door shut, I grabbed Denny by the arm and held on. "Fork it over, Denny!"

"What?"

"You know very well 'what.' That paperweight. The one you swiped from Mrs. Smith."

Denny stuck out his tongue and went "phuut!"—which is his way of like, ignoring the world. I hate it when he does that. He goes "phuut! *phuut!* PHUUT!" all the time a person's trying to talk some sense into him. It's rude and it's messy and spit goes all over.

"That paperweight's valuable, Dennis Ross."

"Phuut!"

"And you can just bet Mrs. Smith isn't going to—"

"Phuut!"

I ducked the spit. "—let us alone. What if she calls the cops?"

"*Phhuuutt!*"

I jammed my pillow over my head and screamed into it. "What if Old Peg *dies*!"

That stopped him right in his size-three pj's. "Dies?"

I threw my pillow on the floor and pounded my fist on the mattress. "It'll be your fault. This is a serious case of animal abuse, Denny. And how can I tell Dad so he can call the sheriff? Mrs. Smith will have you arrested for stealing that paperweight on the slightest pretext. This is *it*. This is big-time trouble. This is serious. You're going to end up like Aunt Mattie always said you would after we turned her into a griffin. In the slammer. In the pokey. In jail. Why in the *heck* did you do it?"

Denny's face turned so red the freckles disappeared. A couple of tears rolled down his cheeks. But he didn't bawl.

And that got to me.

He just said in this scared little voice, "The cat told me told to."

This was so stupid I couldn't ignore it. "You're going to listen to a *cat*! What in the heck does that cat care if you go to jail?" Then: "Don't *do* that Denny," because he wasn't yelling his head off like he does when he's being a real brat, but crying with these serious sobs. "All right, all right, all *right*! I'll fix it. I swear. Just stop that, okay?"

I patted his back, which was hot and sweaty through the pj's. I wiped my hand off on the bedspread, then got a Kleenex from the box I keep on the dresser and dried his face off. One thing I've never figured out is, how come a person's nose runs

so much when you cry? I mean, you cry out of your
eyes, right? Anyhow, I wiped his runny nose and cuddled him a little bit until his freckles came back. I
tried to think like a sensible person.

This didn't have anything to do with magic. Denny
must be having an aberration. An aberration is when
you do something you don't normally do. And nobody
knows why. Like steal paperweights. I'd just have to
tell Dad about Old Peg, that was all, and Mrs. Smith
would tell the cops about my poor brother. If I put
my mind to it, I could think of a way to talk us out
of it. I hoped. I mean, if the government found out
about Denny's magic, they'd probably take him away
to New Mexico or a weird place like that. Like they
do with the guys who find the aliens in *The X-Files*.

A police siren sounded outside, a couple of streets
over, and I jumped. What if Mrs Smith had called
the cops already? I could just imagine what she'd told
them: "The big one had long blond hair, blue eyes,
and a sneaky expression. The short one had red hair
and freckles. She said he was seven years old, but
he's really a dwarf. A dwarf thief. Extremely dangerous."

The police would come up the walk. Ring the door-
bell. Interrogate Denny and me. I would have to say,
"Yes, sir, the cat told him to steal the paperweight."

I started to yell again out of sheer frustration when
it suddenly hit me. I mean, animals do talk to Denny
once in a while. It's part of his being a magician. And
when Denny said that about the cat telling him to
swipe the paperweight, of course I blamed Denny for
actually *doing* it. I mean, a cat doesn't know human

right from wrong. A seven-year-old definitely should.

And actually, thinking back about a lot of stuff, I realized Denny *did* know right from wrong.

I should have trusted him more. I patted him again. His back had cooled off some, so I asked, "Did the cat tell you *why* to steal the paperweight?"

"I didn't steal it!"

Denny was as mad as he'd been when I'd told Mom he'd sold her chocolate-chip cookies to the Girl Scouts. I'd been wrong about that. He'd eaten them instead. Anyhow, I knew a for-real mad when I saw one, so I said in this calm way, "But you've got it. The paperweight."

"Yeah, I've got it. I didn't steal it. I saved it."

"Excuse me? You saved the paperweight? What are you saving it for? And you can't save stuff that belongs to other people. That's called stealing."

"Jeez!" Denny rolled his eyes. "I rescued it."

"Rescued it? From Mrs. Smith? What was she going to do? Drop it? Smash it?"

Denny got that stubborn look. His lips go tight together. Once he even put Scotch tape over them so he wouldn't say a word. At least his freckles were back. I could stop being scared for him and maybe whack him instead.

"Oh, Denneee." I tickled him.

He smacked me in the arm. "You think I'm a crook."

"Denny, I—"

"You *do*! You do, too! I'm not talking to you until you say you're sorry."

So there it was. If I didn't apologize and grovel and

act like a little worm, I wouldn't get another word out of Denny.

"You aren't a crook."

"And say you're really sorry you said I was."

"I didn't *say* you were, Denny. I might have *thought* you were."

"Say you're sorr—"

"Well . . . I'm sorry."

"Are you really really really sorry?"

"Denny!"

"Okay. I did save it. I had to. Belle said so."

"Who's Belle? The cat?"

He grinned at me. "I'll go get the paperweight. Then maybe I can show you, if my magic works. Sit there, okay? Don't move."

"Fine." I settled back on the bed and grabbed Leroy, this stuffed bear I've had since I was about three or something. I only keep it around because it smells good. Plus, right this minute, Leroy kept my hands from grabbing Denny around his skinny little neck. Denny trotted out the door and disappeared. I started to stand up. Denny stuck his head back inside my room and caught me.

"I said sit *there*."

I grabbed Leroy so hard he went "mmmaaa." His squeaker hasn't worked for years. "I'm sitting. I'm sitting."

Denny was back so fast I knew that paperweight had been stored somewhere in his pajamas all along. I grabbed Leroy so I wouldn't punch my little brother out of sheer frustration. He jumped up beside me on the bed and put the paperweight on the comforter.

I hadn't had that much chance to look at it in Zeu-xippe Smith's kitchen. It was beautiful. The golden horse floated in the clear glass, diamond wings moving slowly, ruby eyes clear and honest and bright. Denny put both hands around the crystal. The faintest—just the faintest—little green glow showed at the side of his hands.

This was Denny's magic.

Denny's magic doesn't really work full-time unless we have the pearl necklace and a spell to guide us. So this little bit of his magic, showing up here, showing up now, was a big surprise to me. We bent over the glass, admiring the delicate little horse in its crystal sky. It seemed to move. Its wings flowed up and down. One tiny hoof struck the bottom of the paperweight. A silver ribbon flowed beneath its little foot.

Something whispered. . . .

seeee . . . meee . . . free . . . mee . . . do not go and leave me!

This was astounding!

The winged horse in the paperweight could talk!

three

A WINGED HORSE. A FLYING HORSE. A HORSE THAT spoke poetry.

Pegasus!

I sat up. It was Pegasus!

Where Pegasus struck his foot, poetry flowed like a river! Just like Dad said.

I looked into the jeweled eye of the winged horse. Pegasus. I was looking into the eyes of Pegasus.

The tiny creature circled the glass, neck arched, eyes glowing with a light like the inside of a rose.

The green glow around Denny's fingers went away, slowly, like water down the sink the time I dropped a marble in it. When Denny's magic quit, Pegasus stopped moving. His glittering diamond wings stretched from one side of the glass to the other, as still as a house. The ruby-rose light died away. And the paperweight grew cold.

"The pearl necklace, Denny," I whispered. "I'll get it. Maybe it's time for your magic now. Did you hear what Pegasus said? 'See me! Free me! Do not go and leave me!' That's poetry. Dad said that the real Pegasus is the start of all the poetry in the world. And we've got him right here in this paperweight. Aunt Matty was right when she told us you would have more magical adventures. We can free Pegasus from this spell."

Denny screwed up his face.

"No? You don't want to?"

"Well, yeah, sure." Denny blinked. Maybe because it's always been a part of him—even when it was a hidden part and he didn't know he could use the magic—he doesn't think it's as big a deal as I do. "We *could* use the magic. Except for the witch. I dunno what the witch is going to do. And I'm scared of the witch."

"Holy cow," I said.

It all fell into place. Just like a soccer ball. Right into the goal.

Zeuxippe Smith was a witch!

I mean, it didn't take a diversionary tactic to figure out it would take a witch to capture the only winged horse in the world and stick it into a paperweight. Pegasus, the horse that practically started poetry in this world, for goodness' sake, and she shrank it to this teeny-tiny size and turned it into gold.

Then I thought: If she could do that to a winged

horse—what in the name of goodness could she do to two kids?

Turn him into a pig, she'd said about Denny.

I'd just bet she'd try.

Unless I was going bonkers.

Unless this horse wasn't Pegasus at all.

"Hang on a second, Denny." There was something I had to check about this poetry stuff, first. Just to be sure. I marched out the bedroom door and into the living room. Dad was reading. Mom was watching *Seinfeld,* which has the dumbest jokes of any TV show I know.

"Hello, honey," Mom said. "Is Denny's hair dry?"

"Um. Not quite. Mom?"

"Yes, honey."

"Didn't you have to take poetry in school?"

"I certainly did." She sighed and shook her head. "They don't teach poetry in school nowadays. Not like they used to. Sometimes I wonder what's happened to all the poetry in the world. It seems to have disappeared."

Can you believe this?

She looked over and smiled at Dad. "Remember 'The Raven'? 'Once upon a midnight dreary, while I pondered, weak and weary, over many a quaint and curious volume of forgotten lore . . . '"

" 'At my door I heard a rapping, at my window came a tapping . . .' " Dad said.

Mom shook her head. "That's not right."

"Yes, it is."

"No, it *isn't.*"

I beat it back to the bedroom before I started a divorce. If that was a poem, *we'd* never studied it. So that was *one* poem the witch had swiped, at least. There were probably a lot more. I mean, Mom'd even said they didn't teach poetry in school anymore. That she'd thought it all disappeared. This had to be Pegasus!

"Well?" said Denny, as soon as I got back.

"Mrs. Smith did it. She stole all the poetry in the world. Or most of it, anyway. By capturing Pegasus." I thought a second. If that poem was a sample of what Zeuxippe Smith had stomped out, maybe it wasn't such a big deal to have poetry gone.

"There's poems," said Denny. "There's lots of poems."

"Like what?"

"There's 'I'm a little teapot short and stout, here is my handle here is my spout.'"

"Shut up, Denny. That's not a poem. Not a real poem."

"What is it then."

"It's . . . stuff. Poems should make you feel . . . different. Poems are emotions."

Denny started to go "phuut!" but I slammed my hand over his mouth. "Sad like. Or happy. Or scared. There's a poem I read once—"

"Well, I don't want to hear it," Denny said. "Who cares anyway? And there's no poem that's scarier than that witch."

I picked up the paperweight and shook it. There *were* poems around, that was for sure, but not a whole ton. Maybe the paperweight leaked and just a little poetry came out, compared to the gobs of poetry Mom said was around before schools stopped teaching it. How much would come out if Pegasus were free? I talked to the little horse. "How do we wake you up? How do we get you out? How do we do it without the witch turning Denny into a pig? Or me, for that matter."

"Or Mom and Dad," said Denny. "She could turn Mom and Dad into cows. Or she could cook us and eat us. I'm sacred of that witch."

"Well, I'm not," I said, which was this big lie, "so don't worry."

We had to figure this thing out. I mean, sometimes you sort of wish your folks would take a long vacation because they're kind of nosy and into your stuff, but to have a witch turn them into cows? No way. And I sure didn't want Denny and me to end up witch stew.

It was definitely time for Denny's magic. I reached inside the neck of my T-shirt and pulled out the pearl necklace. I always wear it now, just like I always wear Brian Kurlander's real gold-heart charm. I've worn the pearl necklace ever since our first magical adventure, the time when Denny accidentally turned my aunt Mattie, my cat Bunkie, and his parakeet T. E. into a monster called a griffin. The pearl necklace works with Denny's magic in some way I don't get, yet. One of these days I'll figure it out. What I do know is that without the pearl necklace, Denny can only do little stuff, like getting the Pegasus to move around in the paperweight.

When we work together and I help him with the

necklace, Denny can . . . well, his magic can be awe-some.

I put the paperweight down on the rug and made Denny sit on the other side of it. I put one hand on the pearl, and the other on the top of the paper-weight. Denny stuck his hands around the middle. We both stared into for a long, long time.

Nothing happened.

"Denny? Can you feel anything?"

Denny's eyes were screwed shut. He shook his head. His face got redder and redder, but still nothing happened. I started worrying that I didn't know this magic at all. I don't know how long we sat there, staring at the cold, motionless gold horse, when I heard a scratching at my window.

Bunkie. That good old cat. Mom or Dad must have let her out and here she was wanting back in. I sighed, got up, and went to the window. The windows in this rented house cranked out, so I cranked one side open and called out, "Bunk?"

No cat. Just that scratch-scratch-scratching. And the dark where the moon stayed high and white.

Suddenly I was cold. Even though it was June and like seventy degrees out there. You can never tell about witches. They can sneak up on you in two sec-onds flat. I started to crank the window shut real fast. Suddenly a thin little paw came over the sill, then a scrawny head. . . .

It was the marmalade barn cat. The cat who'd eaten Denny's tuna-fish sandwich.

I cranked the window open wider. That cat strolled in like it owned the place. Tail up in the air, it sniffed around for new or strange stuff. Then it sat in the middle of the rug, its tail curled around its feet.

"Hey," said Denny, and petted its nose.

Belle told me to take it, Denny had said.

"Denny! Is that Belle? Is she talking to you? Can she help us?"

"Belle's not a girl. He's a boy."

"With a name like Belle?"

Denny shrugged. This was ridiculous. First Old Peg was a boy with a girl's name and now this. There's no way a person should call a boy cat by a girl's name. It just goes to show you about witches.

Denny cocked his head to one side, like he does when he's chirping to his stupid parakeet T. E. I hoped this cat wasn't the kind that ate parakeets. T. E. liked to stay in his cage in Denny's room, but sometimes Denny let him fly around the house.

"Belle's hungry," Denny said.

"Is she—I mean he—too hungry to do magic?"

"Yep."

"Sit right there. I'll be back."

Mom and Dad were still in front of the TV when I came through the living room again. Mom was watching *Murphy Brown.*

"Back again?" asked Dad.

"Ah. Yeah. Any liver left, Mom?"

That got her attention. "Yes. Why?"

"I thought I'd get a little snack."

"Of liver?"

"Yeah. As liver goes, it wasn't too bad. Must have been those spices you used."

"I'll have to make it more often."

Great. Liver for life. At least it was better than being stuck in a paperweight for life. Or turned into cows. I looked at them for a second. They were so cute, sitting there. Dad was reading. Mom had on these funny socks she wears to keep her feet warm. I sincerely hoped that cat was going to be able to do some magic after it was full.

I got the liver and walked quietly back to my bedroom and closed the door, just in case *Murphy Brown* wasn't funny enough this week to keep Mom's attention and she decided to see her liver-loving daughter for a bedtime chat.

I wouldn't have believed that poor old Belle had eaten for weeks, much less scarfed down Denny's sandwich that afternoon. He ate that liver between purrs, so it was "purr-gulp, purr-gulp," until it was all gone. He even licked the greasy spot on the rug. Finally, after Belle swallowed the last bit, we put the paperweight between his paws. I held the pearl in one hand, and Denny petted the cat. We waited. And waited.

"Is he saying anything, Denny?"

"Nope."

I sighed. "Does he want more liver?"

"Nope. Look!"

The paperweight began to glow with a light like rising stars. The clear white nudged the edges of the crystal skies. The golden Pegasus lit up like a candle in a dark room.

"Denny!" I whispered. "I recognize that horse! It's Old Peg. A younger Peg, with wings, but it's Old Peg. I swear!"

So *that* was why Old Peg had a girl's name. It was short for Pegasus!

And it *was* Old Peg. The same head, the same muzzle. But Old Peg as he ought to be—wild, free, and flying—with all the poetry of the world flowing from his feet. Not Old Peg as he was now. Skinny as the poor barn cat, and with a drooping head.

Denny's eyes were shut tight. "Pegasus can't get out! He can't get out unless we open the crystal door for him! And she did it. The witch. She captured him and locked his spirit in the paperweight so he'll never fly free."

Belle started to purr. The purr got louder and louder. Denny's eyes began to glow with that magic green. I looked at him, a little scared. "You okay? Do you see anything more?"

"It's something to read. It's under Pegasus' wing."

I got worried. Denny's a pretty good reader for seven, but there's tons of words he doesn't know.

"Wait!" I ran to the dresser and grabbed some paper and a pencil. I had some notepaper I got for Christmas that said FROM THE DESK OF NATALIE ROSS. I could write the spell on that. What Denny couldn't read aloud he could spell, at least. "Okay," I whispered, so as not to disturb the cat. "Spell it out if you can't tell the words."

This is the spell we got:

> First Noble Metals encircle the glass,
> Then Herbs must set fire
> To Heart's Hope from your past.
> As Time speeds on forward,

The glass melts and flows.
And the Wise Poet's freed
As the wind's free
To go.

Awesome. Totally awesome. It must have been pretty powerful magic that we made, too, since Denny didn't have to spell out one word.

"What does the spell *mean*?" Denny asked.

This was a mystery. Usually I like mysteries. I just don't like them when you have to solve them fast to save a starving horse. And from the condition of Old Peg, we didn't have all that much time.

"Well, the wise poet is Pegasus. Dad said that he sprang from the brow of Athena or something."

"Who?"

"Athena. You know, the Greek goddess of wisdom. So it must be Pegasus this spell is talking about. You know, wisdom, Wise Poet."

"No kidding," said Denny, like this was cool. "And all that other junk. About herbs and stuff?"

"Mrs. Smith had herbs in her kitchen. Witch's herbs. Tons of them. We must have to stick them under the paperweight, make a fire, and melt it."

"You can't melt a glass with a fire from some ol' weeds."

"If it's a magic fire, maybe."

Denny shrugged.

I didn't believe this myself, either. "But you remember the way your magic works, Denny."

Denny can push time forward or backward, depending on which way you have to do it. Everything in the universe is made up of molecules. These molecules move. Movement is energy. So everything in the universe has energy. Energy is heat, because when things move, they give off heat. There're these laws of thermodynamics our friend Althea told us about that explain this. One of these laws is all about how if you make molecules stand absolutely still, there's no movement and no heat. This law, called the zero-ith law, says you can't really make things stop moving and have no temperature in real life. But Denny's magic lets him break this law. It's awesome. Denny can make molecules have no temperature. Then he can push them backward, to unmake something, or forward, to dissolve something. This is the same as pushing time forward or backward.

"You can do the time thing. You've done it before with the griffin." I read the spell again. "It's the part about the noble metals I don't get," I said. "I get the part about burning the herbs, but we'll have to find out about noble metals."

"So what is a noble metal? Like a king or something?"

I shrugged. "Ask the cat."

But Belle was asleep, curled in a ball on the rug, his skinny tummy all round with liver. Denny tickled his tail and he growled—some, not loud. "I think that's all the magic Belle can do," Denny said. "Belle's pooped out."

I was about to go look up "noble metals" on my CD-ROM dictionary when there was a tap at my bedroom door. Mom walked in. Dad was right behind her. There was barely enough time to shove the Pegasus paperweight and the spell under the bed. She scooped Denny up, gave him a hug, and saw the little barn cat all at the same time.

"My goodness, Natalie. Where did the cat come from?"

"Through the window," I said, which was the exact and literal truth.

"Oh, dear," Mom said. "Another stray. People in the country can be so cruel sometimes, dropping animals off." She sighed. "I suppose you want to keep her."

"Him," said Denny. "His name's Belle."

"That's a girl's name, honey," Mom said. "You want to give a boy kitty a boy's name."

"His name is Belle," said Denny.

Belle sat up, maybe because he heard his name, and opened his big green eyes. He stared at Denny.

"He's the witch's cat," said Denny the blabbermouth.

What! Now, why in the *heck* did Denny say that?

Dad frowned. "The witch's cat. Do you mean Mrs. Smith?"

"Yeah!"

Belle switched his look to me. A warning sort of look. A look that meant: "Say just the right thing!"

"Natalie?" said Dad, wanting an answer to his question.

"Mrs. Smith's a little weird, Dad."

"What do you mean, 'weird'?"

Now Mom, Dad, *and* the cat were looking at me. Mom and Dad had the *look* look. The kind of look you get in social-awareness class where people talk to you about not getting into a car with strangers.

"Kind of mean. I mean, there was a *ton* of manure to clean up. And it was hot. And she didn't pay us."

"You think the job will be too much work for your brother?"

I looked at Belle. He squeezed his eyes again. So that was what this must be about. Getting Denny out of the witch's way. So I could face her. All by myself. Swell. "Uh, yeah. I do. I think the work's too hard and it's too hot."

"Well, maybe Denny can stay at Bart's when you go back to work. Althea will take care of him."

Belle purred. I like cats, but I wanted to shove this one off my bed and out the window. It was pretty clear good ol' Belle wanted Denny the provider of tuna fish safe and sound.

Denny yawned suddenly. Mom patted him on the back in an absentminded sort of way. "He should be in bed, David. It's been a long day for him. I'll just tuck him in."

Dad waited a second until Mom and Denny went out. "You kids didn't talk much today about the job at Pegasus Farm. How'd it really go?"

"Okay, I guess," I said.

"You both looked pretty pooped at dinner. Did Mrs. Smith treat you guys okay?"

"I guess. Even though, like I said, she was kind of mean."

"Are you going to go back tomorrow?"

"No, Dad." This was out of my mouth automatically. Mrs Smith would want that paperweight, and she knew darn well who'd swiped—I mean rescued—it.

"Did you tell Mrs. Smith you would return, Natalie?"

I didn't say anything. There wasn't anything I *could* say that wouldn't get Denny in trouble with Mom and Dad. Or me, for the crime of Not Keeping Your Word.

Dad put his arm around me and gave me a hug. "It's always good to keep your word, Nat." I knew it! "Even when you might not like the person you've given it to. I get the strong impression that you and Denny didn't like Mrs. Smith all that much. Did she do or say anything to justify your not keeping your word? You know what I mean, honey. You know the difference between right and wrong."

I looked at Belle. He squeezed his eyes shut, then open. Animals don't talk to me like they talk to Denny, but I'd bet anything in this life that the cat wanted me to say something about Old Peg. Just like he'd wanted Denny to call Mrs. Smith a witch so Dad wouldn't let him go back to Pegasus Farms.

For some reason, I trusted Belle.

I decided to tell Dad about that poor horse. I could always say that we'd picked up the paperweight by accident, or something. Or that the heat made Denny bonkers.

Besides, Old Peg was important. Maybe that's what Belle was trying to get me to understand.

"Dad! Mrs. Smith treats that poor horse like . . . like *dirt!* I mean, it was skinny, and starving, and

there were burrs all over the poor thing and that
paddock was gross!"

Boy, that felt good! Like getting a splinter out.

"There wasn't any hay or grain for the horse?"

"Well, yeah, there was. In the back of the shed."

"So there was food on the property?"

"Yeah. All she had to do was *give* it to the poor
thing. She ought to be arrested! It was animal
abuse."

There. It was out.

"Natalie." Dad sat on the edge of the bed. "The law
in New York State is very clear about what consti-
tutes animal abuse. If there's food on the property
and the animal doesn't show physical signs of being
beaten or of an unattended-to illness, there's nothing
to be done."

Was he kidding? "But, Dad!"

"Sorry, Nat. That's the law."

This made me madder than ever. "Then the law's
pretty disgusting!"

"Why don't I come with you tomorrow? Talk to
Mrs. Smith. See this horse for myself. Then we can
decide what to do."

The little cat turned his head away and looked at
the window. I'd swear he was saying no.

"I guess not, Dad."

"You're sure?"

No, I wasn't sure. I wanted somebody else to take
care of this problem. Not me. I wanted to ride Mindy
Blue and take lessons from Uncle Bart's new trainer,
and write letters to Brian Kurlander and have a

summer with no stress. I didn't want to have to deal with witches.

Belle jumped on my lap and reached a paw up to my neck. He tapped the pearl necklace once. Then twice. His paw made it bounce.

Right. *This* must be what Belle wanted me to find out: that the law wouldn't help. Belle wanted me to know that saving Old Peg was up to me. And to the magic.

Denny's magic wasn't just Denny's. The magic was mine, too. It was, like, this awesome responsibility. I knew that.

Jeez!

"Nat?" said Dad.

"You don't need to go over there, Dad. She's not a child molester or anything. So, yeah. I'm sure."

Belle bumped his head under my chin and purred.

"Will you go back to finish the job? I wouldn't like to think that'd you made a decision to bug out on Mrs. Smith just because you don't like her. I don't want you to be a quitter. Finishing what you've started is part of growing up the right way."

The growing-up-the-right-way speech. *Again.* Belle kept on purring. It was pretty loud.

"I can handle it," I said. "Honest." And I could. I hoped.

I mean, this situation was pretty clear now. Even if Dad called the sheriff, what with the horse food on the property and all, nobody would arrest Mrs. Smith. All that would happen is that Denny would get into trouble. So it was up to me. All I had to do was figure out the noble-metal part of the spell. Then

Denny's magic could free Pegasus and everything would be okay.

If the witch didn't get us.

"Well, Nat. Mom and I are going to trust you to do the right thing. Whether you go back or not, it's up to you. We'll stay out of it." He hugged me again and stood up. "Good night, honey."

" 'Night, Dad."

He closed the door behind him, and I was left looking at Belle, that dumb ol' cat with the girl's name.

"Well," I said to him, "I hope you know what you're doing."

He squeezed his eyes shut and then open again.

So. We were on our own, with the paperweight and the spell hidden under the bed. Denny and me and the witch.

And Belle, of course. I hoped *he* really knew what was going on.

CHAPTER

four

I WOKE UP THE NEXT MORNING TO TWO BIG YELLOW eyes staring right in my face. So I sat up straight and yelled. It was good old Bunk, of course, sitting on my chest and wanting food. Bunkie's a great cat, but she has this totally annoying way of waking you up in the morning if she thinks you're sleeping too late. Late to a cat is different from late to a person. The sun was barely up and all these birds were cheeping outside my window. Bunk is used to me sitting up and yelling when she wakes me up, so all she did was jump to the foot of the bed and sit there with her tail curled around her feet. I put the pillow over my head. I could feel Bunk walking over the bedspread. Then I could feel *something else* walking over the bedspread. I sat up with another yell.

It was Belle. He and Bunk were purring at each

51

other, nice as pie. Then they both purred at me. Breakfast, they purred. We want breakfast.

"Oh, all *right*!"

I pulled on a clean pair of jeans and a T-shirt and slammed into the kitchen. It was so early the sun hadn't reached the kitchen yet. Like I said, this house we were in was right next to Uncle Bart's horse farm, which was one of the reasons Mom and Dad had rented it. I could see the barns from the window over the sink. Uncle Bart was up and around already, doing morning chores. I opened a can of cat food and dumped it in Bunkie's bowl. She and good ol' Belle ate side by side. I drank some orange juice and watched them.

"The thing to do," I said out loud, "is to figure out the middle part of the spell. The part about how 'Herbs must set fire to Heart's Hope from your past.' We have to figure out what the heart's hope is. And the noble metal, of course. Then Denny can push time: 'As Time speeds on forward, the glass melts and flows.' If we can solve the mystery of the heart's hope and the noble metal then Pegasus will get out."

Bunk flattened her ears against her head and growled a little bit. She hated having anybody mess up her breakfast by talking. Belle stopped eating for a second and looked at me.

"Right?"

Belle stuck his nose in the food dish. He pushed some of the kibble with his nose and looked up at me again.

Outside the window, Uncle Bart was pushing a big wheelbarrow of hay into the barn. Each of Uncle

Bart's horses got two flakes of hay and a scoop of oats every morning. Some of them, like the big stallion Alternativ, got even more.

Old Peg wouldn't get *any*. Unless I went back to the witch's house.

"I have to get over there and feed Old Peg," I said.

"Meow!" said Belle.

"But if I do, the witch'll see me," I said. "How can I do that and break the spell?" I didn't want to say this aloud, but I was scared of that witch. Maybe I could write an anonymous letter to Uncle Bart. *Horse starving at Mrs. Smith's, go over and feed it.*

Belle jumped up onto the sink and stared out the window. Uncle Bart was leading Mindy Blue and Susie the Shetland pony into the barn for breakfast. In the summer, they stayed out in the paddock at night and came into the barn to eat. They both looked round and shiny.

Not like Old Peg. And Uncle Bart might throw an anonymous letter away.

"I could take Mindy Blue out for a trail ride, I guess," I said to the cats. "Ride her right by that awful shed where's she's got Old Peg and sneak in." An idea hit me. "I could maybe wear a disguise?"

"Meow!" said Belle, like this was smart.

"Yeah. If I were disguised, I could just feed Old Peg real quick, swipe the herbs, and then get the heck out of there."

Belle butted his head against me and reached up with one paw. He patted the pearl necklace where it was lying under my T-shirt.

"Could Denny's magic disguise me?"

Belle growled. My guess was that this meant no. I thought about why and decided Belle was right. Denny's magic was a special kind. He was a nano-magician, which meant that he could rearrange molecules into different shapes. I wasn't sure it'd be all that safe to have my little brother rearrange my molecules into a different shape. I mean, what if he re-arranged me into something gross, like with two heads? And being Denny, he'd forget all about changing me back. I might be stuck for life.

"So I'll disguise myself. I'll disguise myself, and I'll apply for that job at Pegasus Farms just like I did yesterday. Only she won't know that it's me! If she gave me the job—not knowing it was me, of course— I could go there every day and take care of Old Peg. At least until I scope out what the noble-metal and heart's-hope parts of the spell mean so that Denny and I can free him."

This was brilliant, if I do say so myself. "Right, Belle?" I asked. Belle seemed to agree. He purred so loud I thought he was going to vibrate right off of the counter.

"And you know what? I'll disguise myself as a boy."

Belle's green eyes opened wide. Bunkie lifted her head from her dish. I was a little scared, but it should work. I mean, Zeuxippe Smith'd met me for a couple of minutes, tops, yesterday. I'd had my hair down, like I usually do, and there's a lot of it. I could cut that all off, and put on one of Denny's perfectly dis-gusting Terminator T-shirts. And Uncle Bart had a whole collection of caps with football teams plastered all over them. I could pull the hat down over my face and never take it off. A couple of boys at school had hats instead of hair, practically. They never took them off.

I leaned against the sink and thought about how to be a boy.

First off, boys walked like those pigeons in Central Park. Strut. Strut. Strut. Showing off their muscles, most likely. I could do that. I had pretty good muscles from soccer and like that.

Then I remembered this book I read in language arts. *The Adventures of Huckleberry Finn* by some guy named Mark. This Huck Finn wore a dress to fool some people. He got found out because he caught a ball like a boy. Girl push their knees apart to catch things. So if Mrs. Smith threw anything at me, I'd have to remember to stick my knees together.

Boys talked different, too. They talked about hockey and football, blabber-blabber-blabber-blabber until you'd like to die of terminal boredom. And they said stuff like "huh!" and "right!" and "who says?" in a very tough way.

There was a word for the way boys talked, which I knew on account of Dad used it the time I locked Denny in his closet for swiping my CDs. Belligerent. Boys talked belligerent.

"Huh!" I said to Belle the cat, practicing belligerent, "Like, in your face!"

Belle purred and switched his tail.

This was absolutely a plan that would work. And the first thing to do was cut off my hair.

I have to admit, standing in front of the bathroom

mirror, that I didn't know if I could cut off my hair. I'd found a pair of Mom's sewing scissors and stood there, ready to slash.

Last night, when we were talking about no poetry being around, I'd almost told Denny about a poem that made me feel sad and happy all once. I had this poem that made me feel happy. Brian Kurlander wrote it. He gave it to me with this practically solid-gold heart I'd put on my charm bracelet. Absolutely nobody in this world has seen that poem except my best friend Nan. And Madeline. And Annie Dansville. I can shut my eyes any day of the week and recite that poem:

> *Your hair is sunny*
> *Your smile is, too*
> *But not as silky as your hair.*
> *This heart's for you.*
> *I hope your heart is true.*

I guessed from that Brian really liked my hair. I did, too. For a second my hand shook. Just a little bit. Maybe it was longer than a second. But then, it was like poor Old Peg with his clouded eyes and skinny ribs was looking in the mirror behind me.

So I did it.

I cut it all off.

Belle and Bunkie got in the way, making these mewing noises. There were great big chunks of blond hair all over the floor when I finished. Bunkie played with the hair for a little bit until it got up her nose and she started sneezing. Belle just sat on the edge of the sink and meowed when I looked in the mirror. What hair was left stuck up in little feathery spots all over my head.

I decided the short cut wasn't all that awful. It made my eyes look bigger, for one thing. And it'd sure be easier to have short hair in the summertime. Having all that long hair was hot. And I hated it when I got all sweaty from stuff and the hair stuck to the back of my neck. It made me even more hot.

So I don't know how come I cried and cried. No hair's worth the life of a horse.

Pretty soon I stopped crying and went downstairs to breakfast. Mom'd made pancakes and bacon, which was to make up for the liver last night, I guess, and Denny was sitting at the table banging his spoon against his juice glass, waiting for me to get there so we could start eating.

Well. You would have thought I'd been caught pulling wings off baby birds. It was that bad. Mom actually screamed. Then she burst into tears. This made me start crying all over again. Dad drank three cups of coffee real fast and didn't say a word. Denny snickered, the little brat. The commotion was so much that Belle and Bunkie took off like two streaks and disappeared.

"Why?" said Mom after what seemed like hours and hours and *hours* of blubbering. "Darling, *why*? You had just *beautiful* hair. It's the loveliest color I've ever *seen*. You're still beautiful, honey. But your hair. Your hair." She cried again. I bit my lip hard. I thought about Old Peg.

Denny rolled his eyes and asked for more pancakes.

Dad swilled down his third cup of coffee and cleared his throat.

Oh, no, I thought. Here it comes. He's got the Lecture Look.

"Natalie."

"Yes, Dad."

"Is there any—" he stopped. Glared at my mom. Then glared at his plate. "Natalie," he said, like I hadn't heard him the first time, for Pete's sake.

"Still here, Dad."

"This—this haircut. It's not very feminine. You don't—I mean you're not . . ." He threw his hands up. "Allison! Help me on this."

Mom wiped her eyes with her napkin. "What your father is trying to say, honey, is we need to know whether or not you cut off your hair because you don't like being a girl."

Excuse me?

"You know. It makes you look so . . . so . . . boyish."

I mean, that's what I wanted, to look like a boy. Just until I saved Old Peg. Not permanently.

"It'll grow back, Mom. Besides, I like it short. And don't worry. I like being a girl."

"You're sure?"

Jeez!

"I'm sure, Mom."

"I'll tell you what. We'll go into Rochester today and get it styled. Okay? I just wish you *told* me that you wanted it short. If you'd wanted it short, we could have found somebody to cut it . . . well . . . not quite so short."

"It'll be all right, Mom. Is it okay if we don't go to Rochester today? I told Mrs. Smith I'd be back to clean up the rest of the manure."

Denny set down his spoon and opened his mouth and yelled, *"No way!* I'm scared that witch'll turn me into a *pig*!"

I shot a quick glance at Dad. He actually smiled and stopped drinking the rest of that third cup of coffee.

"You don't have to come, Denny. You wanted to stick around Uncle Bart's today anyhow, and maybe ride Susie. Right?"

"I don't want to go back to that witch's house," Denny said. "No way. No way. And she won't even pay us."

"She probably will when I've finished the job," I said. "She even told us she would. And I was the one who told her we'd be back, Denny. I didn't promise for you."

"Darling, your hair," moaned Mom, like being stuck on that was going to solve anything.

"I'm proud of you, Natalie," said Dad gruffly. "I'm proud that you decided to keep your word. But this hair business . . ."

"It's just for the summer," I went on. "And thanks, Dad." And then, in case they really thought I was going psycho and wanted a sex-change operation or something, I said, "I thought my hair'd look cute like this. It makes my eyes look bigger. And if I could wear a little mascara, and maybe some blue eye shadow . . ."

Ha. That got them off are-you-sure-you're-happy-being-a-girl speech fast enough. Unfortunately, it got me right into the no-daughter-of-mine-is-going-to-wear-makeup-until-she's-fifteen speech, which went pretty well, considering.

Breakfast *finally* got over and Mom and Dad went off in the car to tour the Finger Lakes or something. I marched Denny into his room and demanded his high-tops and his Terminator T-shirt.

"No," said Denny, point-blank.

"Yes," I said. "You want to rescue Old Peg, don't you?"

"I won't go back to the witch's house."

"Well, I *have* to. I have to get those magic herbs. I have to feed Old Peg."

"I'm scared of the witch! Aren't you scared of the witch?"

"Heck no, me?" Bet not a lot of boys would say *that* and really mean it. "Look. If you give me your high-tops and your Terminator T-shirt, you won't have to go back to the witch's house. I'm working up a disguise. Mrs. Smith hired a little kid and a girl yesterday, right?"

"So?"

"And today she's going to hire a teenage boy named . . . named . . ."—I thought a second—"named Brian Kurlander. A boy named Brian Kurlander is going to show up and apply for that job."

"Brian's whitewater rafting someplace."

"Denny, you dope. *I'm* going to be Brian Kurlander. Get it?"

"You're gonna be Brian?" Denny blinked. Then he laughed, ha-ha-ha. Then he said in this high squeaky voice he thinks is funny, "Woo-woo Bri-ann." Then: "Natalie's got a boyfriend. Natalie's got a boyfriend." He stopped and this huge grin split his face about half-open. "Natalie is a boyfriend. Natalie's her own boyfriend."

I socked him in the arm. He backed off, rolled on his bed, then started bouncing up and down, which he's not supposed to do on account of it kills the mattress. "You gonna write him a love letter? You gonna tell him you're so in love-love-love with him that you *are* him?"

"Shut *up,* Denny."

Now, Brian Kurlander does write me letters. I write him. Once in a while we even send each other stuff. Like, last week, Brian wrote about how he shot the rapids in a kayak for the first time and he sent me some dried leaves from the forest where they were camping. I kept the dried leaves in a special box in my bedroom along with that poem about my hair. I sent him a picture of me on Mindy Blue in case he forgot what I looked like over the summer. But this love-love-love stuff was just Denny being a bozo, as usual.

"You gonna tell him you cut off your hair?"

I couldn't believe that I got tears again. They did some good. At least Denny stopped jumping on the bed. I sat down on his beanbag chair and pinched my knee so I wouldn't cry. Denny came over and stood next to me. His breath smelled like maple syrup. I felt his sweaty little fingers on my cheek. "I like your hair," he said. "It's cool. It'll be cooler than any girl at school.' "

"It'd better grow out by then," I said. I remembered to clean my nose off on my T-shirt like a boy. Then I cleared my throat. "So. Where're your high-tops? And I need a shirt. One of your super-big ones."

We dug around in Denny's closet for a bit and came up with a truly gross shirt. It had a couple of Power Rangers on it and a puffy decal. When you pressed the puffy decal, the shirt yelled, "Go-go Power Rangers," which was so dumb it wasn't even funny. I pulled the shirt on over my T-shirt.

"It's too small," said Denny. "And your chest sticks out in two little bumps. You look like a girl."

Little brothers are absolutely the worst human beings in the world. I'd already thought about the fact that my chest stuck out. I was going to borrow some of Mom's panty hose and wrap it around myself. But I wasn't about to tell Denny that.

"You wear your shirts too big," I said, which was true. I mean, little kids seem to get off on being totally baggy slobs. "High-tops. Where are they? Come on." I snapped my fingers.

Denny heaved this big, big sigh. He loves his high-tops. I think they're stupid. He thinks they're cool. Which is just like a boy to want these sloppy shoes with the laces dragging. He saved all his allowance for three months and begged for his Christmas and birthday presents combined to get Mom to buy them for him. They're these big boaty things with little lights that come on in the heel when you walk. He wears them flopped open with the laces trailing and thinks he is just *it*.

I jammed my feet into them. Now, I have little feet, which is cool, and Denny has big feet for a seven-year-old. Even then it was squash city with me and those shoes. I could hardly walk. I figured I could wear them in front of Zeuxippe Smith and then take them off and wear my regular sneaks when she wasn't around. All I had to do was get through that first job interview. From the way she talked the first time we'd met her, she wasn't down at poor Old Peg's pen very much.

"Okay," I said. "Now we have to get a pair of Dad's pants."

"Dad's *pants*? You're gonna wear Dad's *pants*?"

"Denny! What is absolutely the coolest thing the big boys wear at school?"

"Oh. Yeah. Baggies."

"Right. And your baggies on me are going to look like regular chinos. So we'll get some of Dad's and cut the legs off."

"Are you serious? He'll kill you."

"I'll tell him I mangled them in the washer or something."

We went into the laundry room and dug a pair of chinos Dad wears to paint stuff out of the laundry basket. I tucked a pair of Mom's panty hose into my jeans pocket and just said, "Shut-up, shut-up, shut-up," when Denny started bugging me about them. I got the sewing scissors again and whacked off the bottoms of Dad's pants. I pulled them on over my jeans. They bagged just fine.

The final thing was the spell. I dug that out from under my bed, where we'd hidden the paperweight. Then I stuffed everything into one of those plastic bags from the grocery store: Dad's pants, Mom's panty hose, Denny's shirt, the high-tops, and the paperweight. I stuffed the spell in my jeans in case I had to read it again.

"You ready, Denny?"

Denny's eyes got big. "I have to come?"

"No, stupid. How could I disguise you? Unless you want me to glue some of my cut-off hair to your head and make you into a girl."

I seriously considered this while Denny was squalling and screeching and going, "Ick! Ick! *Ick!*" Then I figured it might be too much of—what d'ya call it?—a coincidence. It'd be too much of a coincidence that a big girl and a small boy showed up for a job interview one day, and a small girl and a big boy showed up the next.

"Never mind. You'd just blow our cover. I'm going to leave you at Uncle Bart's with Althea, just like we told Mom and Dad. Then I'm going to saddle up Mindy Blue and ride over there and take care of Old Peg."

"Why don't you ride your bike?" said Denny. "Bikes are more cool than horses."

I tucked the bag with the pants, shirt, high-tops, panty hose, and paperweight into a bundle and stuck them under my arm. "For one thing, stupid, Zeuxippe Smith might recognize my bike. It's a girl's bike, remember. And for another thing, bikes are *not* cooler than horses."

"They are so," said Denny.

"They are not," I said back. This really dumb argument continued all the way over to Uncle Bart's. We found him, John Ironheels, and Althea mucking out stalls.

Uncle Bart is my mom's youngest brother. He's got a tanned face and bright blue eyes like Mom's. For as long as I can remember, he's had this great horse farm in upstate New York at Cayuga Lake near Lake Ontario. He takes his horses to show in dressage competitions all over the country. Dressage is like horse ballet, where the horses do dancey movements like collected canters and extended trots. You have to be a really good rider to do it.

Our friend Althea Brinker is pretty cool, too. Most of the time she's a graduate student at Columbia University in New York. She stays with us when Mom and Dad go on trips for their advertising-agency clients. She's a tutor, too, and helps me out in subjects like geography, where I get bored and don't do so well. I get good grades in science, so a lot of times she tutors me in science stuff I wouldn't get until I was a senior, for Pete's sake. Anyhow, she was staying at the farm this summer to help out Uncle Bart, and also to tutor me in geography, which, like I said, is not my best subject. I mean, who cares what the capital of Wichita is?

The one thing about Althea is she's got great hair. It's long and red and curly. When I saw her with a big shovel load of fresh sawdust for the horse stalls, I almost started crying about my own hair again.

She saw Denny and me. Opened her mouth. Closed it.

And didn't say one little word. Which is one of the great things about Althea. She knows when to shut up. She'd known for a while about Denny being a magician, but right after our first adventure she forgot all about it. I don't understand this part of the magic.

John Ironheels is Uncle Bart's barn manager, and he used to know about Denny's magic, too. I was sure he'd forgotten, just like Althea and our aunt Matty had, but once in a while he'll look at Denny with a small smile on his face. Then I wonder. There's more to John Ironheels than you'd think.

John didn't say anything about my hair either, but John doesn't talk much any day of the week. Uncle Bart was driving the tractor with the manure spreader attached when Denny and I walked into the barn. He was wearing a hat with "Buffalo Bills" stitched on the front. This is a football team from somewhere around here that he likes.

I said hi.

He said, "My *God,*" then: "Natalie, what the heck did you do to your hair! Does your mom know about this?"

"I *was* thinking maybe I could borrow your hat," I said, trying to be cool and, like, joke about it.

"I think it looks terrific," said Althea. "How are you guys? I didn't see you at all yesterday. You want to get together for some tutoring this afternoon, after the jumping clinic?"

"Yeah!" said Denny. "I want to do it instead of the clinic."

"You aren't invited to the jumping clinic, Denny. But I'll be there, Althea."

"Thea," said Uncle Bart, who tends to get stuck on like, one teeny tiny point, "she looks like a boy!"

That was the idea, wasn't it?

"John, did you see Natalie's *hair*?" said Uncle Bart, like it wasn't totally obvious to the whole universe I was practically bald. Uncle Bart has a hard time getting off a subject sometimes.

"Yes." John gave me a small, quiet smile. "It's her choice Bart, isn't it?"

"Well, yeah, but gee, Natalie. What d'ya have there? You carrying your hair wrapped up in a bag?"

I grabbed the bundle a little tighter. "Just some riding stuff."

"It's not your hair, then?"

Jeez!

"She looks fine," said Althea. "Just fine. Just give her your hat, Bart."

Uncle Bart gave me the hat.

I stuck it on. It came so low over my face I practically couldn't see. I shoved it back.

Althea said, "So what are you guys up to today?"

"I thought I'd take Mindy Blue out for a trail ride," I said. "Denny wants to hang out here."

"Brandy'd like that," said Althea. Brandy was Uncle Bart's dog. She's a golden retriever, and except for the fact that she likes to chase Bunkie once in a while, she's great.

Althea winked at me and said, "Come on, Mindy's just finished her breakfast. Be sure not to ride her too hard the first hour, okay? So she'll have a chance to digest her food."

I wanted to hop on Mindy Blue, gallop over to Mrs. Smith's, and give poor Old *Peg* a chance to digest some food. But I said, "Okay." There're things about horses you can't push.

Althea and I went over to Mindy Blue's stall. Mindy is a chestnut quarter horse. She has a white blaze on her nose and a little white sock on her left hind leg. She has a very calm, sweet personality. She's very sensitive to being handled by a person. Uncle Bart won't let anybody but me ride her in the summer. Only advanced riders in his classes can use her when I'm not there. So even though I wanted to race off and save Old Peg, I got Mindy ready for our ride in the right way. Horses aren't the least little bit like cars or bikes. Uncle Bart says they're the "other beings" in our universe. They deserve respect.

My heart was hammering a little bit now that I was getting ready to go. I sure *was* scared of Zeuxippe Smith.

Mindy Blue knew that something was wrong. I snapped her halter on, drew her out of the stall, and put her in the cross ties to get her ready to tack up. She kept bending her head around to look at me with this question on her face. You know that a horse is asking a question when its upper eyelids crinkle in a little triangle and it puts its ears forward.

I got out the rubber currycomb from the tack box. I brushed the dust out of Mindy's coat with circular rubbing motions. Then I smoothed her with the body brush. I combed out her mane and tail. I got a damp sponge and wiped her nose and eyes. I looked around to see if anyone was noticing. I stuck the combs and brushes in my bag with my boy's clothes. I'd give Old Peg a good grooming today.

If Mrs. Smith didn't turn me into a frog.

I decided to use a western stock saddle on Mindy Blue, in case I had to get away fast from Pegasus Farms. The stock saddle has a deep seat and a horn in front that cowboys tie ropes to. The horn is good for hanging on if you're racing over rough country. Like in a race away from a witch.

Mindy Blue stuck her nose in my side and pushed hard. She still had that question on her face.

"It's okay, girl," I said. Then: "Easy, easy," as I cinched up the girth. Some horses, like Uncle Bart's smart old mare Scooter, hold their breath when you cinch them up and inflate their bellies. When you go to get on, the horse lets its breath out and *whump!* The saddle slides right around. You are on the ground. Mindy doesn't do that, but after I put the bridle on and led her out of the barn, I checked the cinch anyhow. It was nice and snug. Two-finger snug, Uncle Bart calls it, which means you can just barely wriggle two fingers between the horse's side and the cinch.

The stock saddle has rawhide strips hanging down from the fenders so that cowboys can tie bedrolls and stuff to the horse. I tied my rolled-up disguise to

Mindy Blue, then mounted. I adjusted Uncle Bart's Buffalo Bills hat so that I could see. Althea came out of the barn to wave good-bye. She called, "Have a good ride!"

I nodded and waved back. I thought if I said anything, my voice would croak, so I just gave her a big grin. There must have been something wrong with the grin. She called out, "Are you all right? You'll be back in time for the clinic, won't you? You have to see this guy Bill ride. He's terrific!"

Mindy backed up fast and snorted. I must have squeezed my knees into her without realizing, since she's very obedient to the cues you give her when you ride. "I'll be back," I called. This time I squeezed Mindy Blue the right way, by tapping both heels lightly against her sides.

We were off across the pasture.

Headed to the house of the witch.

CHAPTER

Five

IT WAS ONE OF THOSE GREAT SUMMER DAYS IN UP-
state New York. The sun was shining. The flowers
were out and all that. Uncle Bart's horse farm has
apple orchards on the side that goes down to Lake
Ontario. The orchards belong to Amos Barker. His
trees were full of baby apples. The summer smelled
great.

Big grass paths run between the trees so Mr. Barker's picker trucks can go down when the apples are
ready for harvest. The paths are great for riding. It
was a lot faster to cut through one of Mr. Barker's
groves on those grassy paths. Mindy Blue stepped
right along. We got to the creek that flows to the lake
where I'd planned to change into my disguise.

I dismounted and looped her reins over the branch
of an apple tree. Between trying to get Mom's panty

hose wrapped around my chest to flatten it like a boy's and trying to keep Mindy from eating those little green apples, I got too busy to be scared about meeting the witch.

I finally got everything on. Dad's pants were the biggest pain. They hung just below my knees. I had to bunch the material around the waist and sort of mash my belt over it. Plus the button was on the wrong side. This made no sense to me at all. How come girls' button are on the left side of clothes and boy's are on the right? Anyhow, Denny's Power Ranger sweatshirt would cover the pants.

I was almost ready, but boy, was I hot. Then I thought to myself, I should say, "Girl, was I hot," since I was making this switch from girl to boy.

I dipped my hands in the creek and slicked my hair back. It felt weird, bringing my hands to the back of my head and finding no hair. I almost cried again. I don't mind crying, myself. If you have to be sad, crying's the best way to get rid of it.

Now, one thing about boys is very weird. After about sixth grade they don't cry as much as girls. As least, I never see them. Dad says in other places boys cry more than girls. Like in Arabia or someplace like that.

Then I wondered if in Arabia boys catch balls the same way girls do here. If they cried like American girls, maybe they caught baseballs the same way as American girls. If Mrs. Smith had spent a lot of time in Arabia, I was in big trouble pretending to be a boy. I hoped she hadn't. I hoped she'd just been an American witch, and just knew about American boys.

I put on the baggy pants and disgusting Power
Ranger shirt. I jammed my feet into Denny's high-
tops. I slicked my hair down again with water and
stuck the Buffalo Bills cap on. "What do you think
about my disguise, Mindy Blue?"

Mindy Blue, trying to get to another apple, totally
ignored me. I grabbed her reins and pulled her to the
creek. I could see my reflection in the water.

I looked really, *really* strange.

"My name's Brian Kurlander," I said in the deepest voice I could make. "I'd like to apply for this job
you advertised. In the supermarket."

"I see, Mr. Kurlander," I said back to myself in a
witchy, mean voice. "What are your qualifications for
this job?"

"I'm a hard worker, ma'am."

"And what else?" I tried to make the witch's hiss.
"Do you know about horssssesss?" I made a horrible
face in the water.

I got depressed. I didn't look like any boy on the
face of this earth. Whether he was from Arabia or
Africa or Afghanistan. It wasn't going to work. I wondered if I knew anything about being a boy for sure
or if I was just guessing.

Two men in a fishing boat floated around the bend
in the creek with their fishing poles over the side.

"Hey, boy!" shouted one of the men from the boat.
"Get that horse away from them apple trees!"

I jumped about a foot.

"You hear me? Them's my apples."

It was Mr. Barker, the apple farmer next to Uncle
Bart's. I'd known him all my life, practically. Mr.

Barker rowed the little boat close to where I was standing. "What you doin' there, boy?"

"Just out riding," I said in my Brian Kurlander voice.

Mr. Barker squinted at me. "That's one a' Bart Franklin's mares you got there. Where'd you git it?"

"Unc—I mean Mr. Franklin said I could ride her, sir."

"Hah. One them students of his? Boys shouldn't be doin' sissy ridin' like that." He let the oars rest. These two guys floated in the water, watching me. I decided they were both dumb for saying that dressage was sissy riding. I watched them back.

"He shoulda tole you to stay away from my apples."

"Yessir. Sorry, sir."

"All right, then." He started to row down the creek. "Pretty polite for a kid," I heard Mr. Barker say to the guy in the boat with him. "Most boys today ain't worth a bucket a warm spit."

I patted Mindy Blue and tried not to grin like a fool. It worked! The disguise worked!

"Except for the polite part," I said to Mindy Blue. "Boys are ruder than girls, I guess. In America." Which might be kind of interesting, being rude. I should have thought about this before. Denny was practically the rudest kid in the universe and he was a boy.

Maybe this was going to be fun.

Trying to be a boy didn't seem like as much fun as all that the closer I got to the witch's house. The closer I got, the more I thought about it. Whatever made boys different from girls, it wasn't clothes. It wasn't the way you caught balls. It wasn't whether you belted people in the mouth or not. It wasn't even hair. I could think of too many boys who wore long hair and who didn't smack other kids. I could think of too many girls who liked baggy T-shirts and baggy jeans. There were just a couple of things that were like permanently different as far as I could tell.

Hair, for instance. Some boys had mustaches. Maybe I should have pasted some of my cut-off hair on my upper lip.

Another thing was rudeness. Boys were rude. They spoke belligerently. Boys' buttons were on the wrong side of their clothes. Their voices were lower. Their chins stuck out. And they had bigger noses. And they didn't grow up and get pregnant. Trying to be a boy didn't seem to be all that safe a disguise, since most of the things that made boys different from girls you couldn't see. If Mom's panty hose slipped off my chest, the witch would see I was a girl right away. The witch wouldn't be able to see that the button on Dad's pants was the right way for a boy, either, which was the only truly boylike thing I had on.

I definitely wanted to go back being a girl as soon as I saved Old Peg. If it hadn't been for that starving horse, I would have given the whole thing up and just gone back to being me, Natalie Ross. This whole what's-a-boy thing was way too confusing.

I didn't want to trot Mindy Blue since she'd just had her breakfast, so I made her walk slower and slower the closer I got to Pegasus Farms. Because I was coming crosslots, I came to Mrs. Smith's crummy house first, instead of like yesterday, when we had come from the road.

I reined in Mindy Blue and sat there, looking at it. My stomach felt like about five hundred turtles were swarming around in it. I could just see the shed where Old Peg was beyond the trees. Mindy Blue lifted her head and whinnied hello, like horses do when they meet. I heard Old Peg whinny back. A clear call, like a trumpet. That did it. That good old horse deserved some help.

I squeezed my knees and Mindy Blue walked forward.

The house was quiet.

I got off Mindy Blue and walked up to the front door, tramping like Clint Eastwood does. Brain Kurlander didn't tramp, but then, he was only fourteen. I decided I shouldn't have tried to disguise myself as a boy. I should have tried to disguise myself as a very short adult.

The reins were slippery in my hands. I wiped one hand, then the other, down the sides of Dad's pants. I tied Mindy Blue to the rickety railing and tramped up to the front steps.

Bang! The door flew open. Zeuxippe Smith stood there, looking as weird as ever, her little eyes glittering red in the sun.

"What?" she demanded.

I kept my voice low. That was one thing I was sure of. Boys had lower voices than girls. I hoped like heck my voice wasn't going to shake. "Come about the job," I growled, just like Clint Eastwood in those cool westerns. I shifted from one foot to the other. Clint

Eastwood would've spit on the ground. I tried to work up some spit, but my mouth was dry.

"A fine strong boy like you?"

Whew!

She came down the steps. She didn't walk like a person did with her knees bending and all. She sort of rolled. I wondered what was under that long black skirt she wore. Lizard legs? I started to laugh. I turned the laugh into a cough. Once I started laughing, I'd probably laugh and laugh and laugh until my hat fell off and she could see I was a girl. I mean, my nose and chin had no hair on them.

"I could use a strong boy like you. A poor widow woman like me." The jewels on her fingers flashed in the sunlight.

"What's the job?" I was going to add "ma'am," which Clint Eastwood would've said. Then I remembered about boys being rude. "The ad said a stable hand."

"That's what I want. A nice steady boy to help out around the farm. Are you stable, boy?"

What the heck? Then she cackled hee-hee-hee. I wondered how come I hadn't realized she was a witch right away.

"Yes, ma'a—I mean, yeah."

"I have a horse. The shed where the horse lives needs to be cleaned out. But most of all, most of all, I need an apprentice."

I didn't say anything. I wasn't all that sure I knew what an apprentice was.

"Now, I've had several applicants for the job. Several. So it's a desirable job. A fine job. And I've had so many applicants, I've been wondering whether or not I should even pay them."

"Somebody else has got the job?"

"I've had to fire a few," said Zeuxippe Smith. "Just yesterday. A perfectly horrible little girl and a brat she said was her brother. Sssssssahh!" She made a hissing sound, like a snake. Mindy Blue threw her head up and backed up the length of the reins. "I should have turned them into *pigs*! They were thieves. They stole from me. And they kidnapped my cat. But never mind. You don't want to know about that. What are your qualifications?"

I was ready for that one. "I work hard."

"Ver-rry good." She smiled that creepy smile. "Very well. I shall hire you as my apprentice. Do you know what an apprentice is?"

"No."

"First you will clean out that shed. Then you will come to the house and help me . . . brew."

"Brew? Like coffee?" I can make coffee.

"No. Brew wonderful things. Cook them and stew them and brew them. I make fine herb jams. Excellent herb jellies. Those sorts of things. I need an apprentice. To teach certain parts of my craft." She climbed the staircase of the porch, taking a step on each word. "And. Just. To help."

My mouth was suddenly full of spit after all. I swallowed, hoping like heck she didn't see how nervous I was. She wanted me to hang out in the kitchen? I'd have to stand close to her? Then I remembered the middle part of the spell, about the herbs. I needed a chance to stick some in Dad's pockets.

But which herbs? She had about a million of them.

If I was the witch's apprentice, maybe I could find out.

"Here is the key to the pen," she said, tossing it to me. I remembered just in time to catch it like Dad catches a baseball and Huck Finn, too, or *wham!* the disguise was off. Unless this witch had spent time in Arabia. "You get that shed cleaned out. Then come back up here." She smiled that no-smile. "And then? Return here. I may even have some . . . cookies . . . for you."

"Not real hungry, ma'am."

"A polite boy! An agreeable boy! How nice! How lucky! Yes, my luck is in today."

I hoped my luck was, too.

Mindy Blue and I walked on down to the shed. Old Peg heard us coming, of course. He was waiting with his head up and a happy look. You know a horse is happy when its lower lip is sort of floppy and it makes low, chuckling sounds when you get near it.

I tied Mindy Blue to the outside of the fence. She went to sleep in the sun. Then I went into the pen. First, I refilled the water bucket with good clean water from the pump. I let Old Peg drink that right down. Then I gave Old Peg two flakes of that good hay and a medium-size scoop of oats. I worked on the paddock while he was eating.

Denny and I had done more than I thought. Pretty soon the little area where Old Peg could walk around was nice and clean. Then I got out the brushes and the combs and went to work cleaning this horse up. Old Peg loved the currycomb and the brush. I combed all the burrs out of his mane and tail.

I went to work on his feet. Uncle Bart says this all the time: "No foot, no horse." Which means if you don't take care of your horse's feet, he'll go lame on you, and there you are, you can't ride or anything. Plus it's terrible for the horse. You work on a horse's feet by taking the hook pick and cleaning out the dirt and stones and manure away from the toes. You have to ask the horse to lift his feet so that you can do this. You ask a horse to lift its feet by standing next to him, looking the same way the horse is. Then you put your hand on the leg you want the horse to pick up. Then you bend down while running your hand down its leg. The horse will pick up its foot. Then you can hold the hook and use the hoof pick.

You have to pick a horse's feet out every day. And you have to have the horseshoer come every two months and clip the horse's hooves so they don't grow too long. Old Peg's hooves weren't too long, but they were packed with dirt and stone. It took me a long time to clean it all out with the hoof pick. At least he didn't have thrush. Thrush is this gross infection that comes from not cleaning your horse's feet out and letting him stand in manure. When you look at the inside of the hoof, you can see that the spongy part in the middle is all swollen. There is an absolutely terrible stink. The spongy part of Old Peg's hoof was kind of dried up. I bent over and it smelled like dirt, so that was okay.

I kept hoping maybe Belle would show up for company, but he never did.

After this really, really short time, there wasn't anything else to do. Except go up to the house and try this apprentice stuff.

I brushed Old Peg a second time. Combed his mane and tail again. Then walked around the little paddock looking for any stray bits of straw or stuff that I could sweep out.

Finally, there wasn't a thing more that I could do except go back up to the house.

"I'll be back tomorrow," I said to Old Peg.

He looked at me, sympathetic-like.

"Unless I get turned into a chicken or whatever."

He snorted. He nodded yes.

Yikes!

"You think I'm scared to go up there, don't you?"

Old Peg snorted.

"Well, maybe I won't get turned into a chicken. Maybe I'll just outsmart you-know-who. I've got this job. I can come every day and feed you until I . . ." I looked around. You never knew where that witch was going to turn up. "Until I find out . . . you know. How to break the spell."

Old Peg snorted. He nudged me with his nose. He gave a happy sigh. You know a horse is giving a happy sigh when it blows out "paahh," with a contented sound.

I went out of the pen, got on Mindy Blue, and rode to the witch's house. The turtles in my stomach were back, big time. Mindy felt this. She jibbed all the way up to the porch. I would have jibbed, too, if I hadn't been in disguise. I tied her to the front-porch rail. Petted her a good long while. Then decided I'd better go find out about being an apprentice.

I went to the back door this time, and peered in the window, like I did before. Yep. All those herbs were on the shelf and that square pot was boiling away on the stove. I slouched like a boy and picked my nose, which is what rude boys do. In America.

Bang! The back door flew open.

I waited.

No Zeuxippe Smith.

The kitchen yawned in front of me. Like a giant black mouth waiting for Natalie Ross stew.

Was I supposed to go in, or what? Me, Natalie, I would have waited around to be invited in. Bruce Willis would've walked right in and hollered, "Yo!"

Which is what I did.

Still no witch. I kept myself from looking over my shoulder. Well, there were herbs in that old spell and I was standing in front of a bunch of them. I stuck my hands in the pockets of Dad's pants and started to look at all the stuff.

Somebody had labeled the bottles in a tidy handwriting. I dug the spell out of my pocket. It didn't say what kind of herbs I should be looking for. I bet the herbs had to do with horses. So I started looking for horse herbs. Some were like the regular old herbs Mom uses to cook with: basil, oregano, chives, parsley, and like that. Others were weird: self-heal, heartsease, comfrey, borage. Still others were just plain disgusting: bloodroot, wound wort, lungwort, and wormwood.

Then I found the shelf with what had to be the right herbs. A little sign said SPECIALS, just like in the grocery store. The bottles were square, like the pot. The labels on the bottles were written in letters that changed color in the kitchen's dim light. Now red. Now black. Now red again. Not like any grocery store I've ever been in. These herbs were:

Horse-bane
Horse-wound
Horse-wort
Horse-nip

There was even a horse-relish, which like, totally freaked me out. I stared at the relish pretty hard. The relish didn't *look* like ground-up horse, but you never knew with a witch.

"So, my fine strong boy!"

Jeez!

There she was, standing by the stove.

I crumpled the spell up quick. I shoved my chin down. I looked at her from under Uncle Bart's hat. "I'm done," I said gruffly.

"Good. Gooood. Now, that big pot there. The one in the corner. It must be filled with water. *Not* from the sink, stupid! From the creek, outside. It must be groundwater and never have touched iron. Take the ladle, there. *No!* Not the copper one! The one of glass. If you break it . . ." Her teeth flashed. I gasped.

They were pointed. Like a snake's fangs.

". . . I say if you break it." She leaned forward. She squealed, "Oink. Oink. Oink."

She'd turn me into a pig. I don't know why it is, but a lot of witches I've read about like to turn people into pigs. I decided if I was going to risk being turned into an animal, I'd just as soon it was a dog, or, of course, a good ol' horse. Maybe if she caught me and discovered I was really Natalie Ross, I'd have time to make a request.

I wondered if boys had more guts than girls. Would a boy say, like, "Yo! So! Like, I'd rather be a cat." This would make the witch cross. I figured most people had more sense than to make a witch crabbier than she already was. Whether they were boys or girls.

"Stop daydreaming and *get going*!" hissed Zeuxippe Smith.

That big old pot was heavy. I lugged it outside and carried it down to the part of the little creek that ran through Zeuxippe Smith's farm. The glass ladle she'd made me take was cloudy and thick. It didn't hold much water. It took me a long time to fill the pot. A lot of the water splashed out when I dragged it back. So she made me take it back to the creek. I emptied it and started all over again. I started to get mad. Being mad is better than being scared out of your wits, but not by much.

Finally, I got that darn pot filled the way she wanted it. I heaved it up on the stove. "The herbs must boil," she said. So I had to carry wood in to feed the stove so that the fire would be nice and hot. So I hauled and I hauled and the fire leaped higher and higher and that kitchen got hotter and hotter. The darn herbs never boiled! *I* was boiling in Denny's Power Rangers sweatshirt.

Finally the pot started boiling, too. It was afternoon now, way past lunch. I was so starved, I bet I would have eaten those cookies the witch was always talking about, if she'd offered me any. Which she didn't. I was starved, mad, and tired. It was getting so late I was afraid I was going to miss my riding clinic.

"Are you going to make the herb jellies now?" I asked, hoping like heck she wasn't.

"Yes. Finally! Now that you've done what I said."

" 'Cause if you are, I'll help. But not today. Maybe tomorrow?" Helping her make her disgusting herb jellies was the safest way I could swipe some of those horse herbs. I could pretend to be dumb and bring her the wrong ones and I'd get a chance to stick some in my pockets while I was putting them back on the shelves.

Her beady little eyes narrowed. "A boy? Cooking? That's women's work!"

Excuse me? This was so stupid I almost forgot about her being a witch. I mean, one of our big things Sundays in Manhattan is Dad teaching Denny how to make pancakes. Boys *act* different than girls, but they can do exactly the same things. But I didn't, of course, forget that she was a witch and say this.

"Uh, yeah," I said, keeping my head down. "But cooking's, like, cool, y'know? So maybe tomorrow I could help."

"Tomorrow," she said, and hissed. "Yessss. Tomorrow. You'll be back, tomorrow. Right, my boy? To help make the jellies that I'm cooking." She came closer, closer. Her tongue flickered in and out of her mouth. Like a snake's. "The jelly that I'm cooking is going to need—" She leaned closer as she talked and felt my arm. Her hands were dry and scaly. She interrupted herself, which bugs me. I mean, if people are going to threaten you, they should, like, just do it. "My! You're a stringy boy, aren't you? We'll have to fatten you up!"

"We're going to need what, Mrs. Smith? For the herb jellies?"

Then she hissed, so quietly I could hardly hear, "*Meat.* Soon we add the meat. Perhaps—in a few days' time. Then, little man, you can help. Oh yes. You can certainly help cook!"

I was worrying about whether to say I had to leave when the witch said, "Out, boy," just like I was a dog or whatever, then: "You can go. Be here tomorrow."

Swell. I nodded, backed out of the kitchen, and untied Mindy Blue, trying not to move too fast, in case Zeuxippe Smith could see how scared I really was.

Once on Mindy's back, I felt a lot safer. We galloped back down to Old Peg to say good-bye. I gave him another couple of flakes of hay and some oats. The sun was all the way over to the other side of the sky, and he looked almost shiny in the afternoon light. His head was up. And his eyes looked clearer. You could still see his poor old ribs sticking through his coat. At least he wasn't all covered with burrs and dirt. The pen looked good, too, all raked and clean. I picked up another couple of piles of manure he'd left during the day. Then Mindy and I turned and headed for home. Fast.

Meat . . . The witch's voice rang in my ears as we cantered along. *Soon we add the meat!*

I actually felt those scaly fingers on my bare arm. And shivered.

CHAPTER

Six

I RODE OUT OF THE WITCH'S YARD LIKE LIGHTNING. IT was close to two o'clock, the time for my clinic lesson with Uncle Bart's new trainer.

I stopped Mindy Blue as soon as we caught sight of the barns beyond the apple orchards, changed back into my Gap jeans and T-shirt, and pulled my own boots on. What a relief! Walking around in Denny's high-tops had squinched my toes something awful. Plus, I was getting big-time blisters on my heels. Then I dug my hand into Dad's pants to put the spell back into my jeans.

It was gone.

I, like, panicked.

I checked Dad's pants again. I shook out that dumb Power Rangers shirt. I even checked Denny's high-tops, thinking maybe it had gotten stuck in my shoes.

No soap. No luck. No spell.

Did the witch have the spell? And if she did . . . *did she know who I was?*

The notepaper. That darn notepaper. It said FROM THE DESK OF NATALIE ROSS right across the top.

I shivered. Seventy-three degrees on a nice June day, and I was shivering.

Did Zeuxippe Smith mean the same thing about my stringy arm that Mom did when she complained about buying stringy chicken?

I rode Mindy Blue as fast as I could back to Uncle Bart's, trying not to think about it. Or the square pot, which was a pretty big pot. About the size of a chopped-up fourteen-year-old.

Well, there wasn't a thing I could do about it. If that witch did have the spell, and if she suspected me of being the one who had her precious old paper-weight, and if she did know who I was—well, I was just plain out of luck. I just had to hurry up and use Denny's magic to free Pegasus. Fast.

But to do that, I had to figure out the part in the spell about the heart's hope and the noble metal. And I was, like, *clueless*.

I tried to calm down. I thought about this clinic I had to be at in twenty minutes. I needed to be pretty tidy for that. And I looked a mess.

I checked out getting back to being a girl by looking in the river. My hair was an absolute total mess. My face was all grubbed up. I hoped this Bill Fromm didn't want his students as neat as the horses were supposed to be. Horse people have this saying about horses that were a total mess: "He's been rode hard and put away wet." I guess it's about the worst thing you can do as a horse person is to ride your horse hard and put it away wet. I took out the brushes and combs I used on Old Peg and tried to make my hair look okay. The brushes left little bits of Old Peg's silvery hair in mine, so I gave that up.

I wasn't really in the mood to do the clinic anyway, being so worried about the witch. The best thing to do was act normal. Normally, I'd be really happy I was going to learn to jump. So I thought about that. I'd been really psyched about this Bill Fromm, who was going to teach me how to jump fences. I even began to get a little bit excited. Mindy Blue was a pretty good jumper. But the highest I'd ever jumped was eighteen inches. Anybody could do that. I wanted to jump three feet. Mindy Blue could do it. So could I, if this Bill Fromm was as good a teacher as everybody said.

Mindy Blue was anxious to get back to the barn. I had to be careful and walk her the last few hundred yards to the barns. I didn't want *her* to look like she'd been rode hard and put away wet. Horses love their food, and the place where they get their food is their stalls, so they start to run as soon as they sniff home. So I got even sweatier and tireder than I was from working at the witch's house.

I walked Mindy Blue into the brick yard in front of the barns. I started to feel pretty good. I'd done it! Old Peg was getting better. The witch wanted me to come back. I'd probably dropped that spell when Mindy Blue and I were galloping away from there. For a second I felt like, Yay! Witch: 0, Kids: 1.

Life was swell. Even if I didn't have any hair.

I patted Mindy Blue and made up a little song in time to her walk.

> "I got the witch
> We're gonna jump
> I'm going to fly
> She'll take a bump."

That great mood lasted about thirty seconds. That jumping clinic was the worst experience of my entire life.

It was like this: I got to Uncle Bart's just as the other students for the clinic were riding around in the ring. Althea was up on Uncle Bart's big stallion Alternativ. Alternativ is the most incredible horse in the universe. He's black and silky. He looks like a movie star. Althea looked gorgeous, too. Everybody but me looked fabulous, all neat and clean in breeches and helmets and white shirts with the stocks neatly tied.

"You're late, Nat," called Uncle Bart. "Out looking for your hair?"

Ha-ha.

He came closer. "Wow, kid."

I hate it when people call me kid.

"What have you been up to? You look like you've been rode hard and put away—"

"Don't, Bart," said good old Althea. "You do look like you've been working hard, Natalie. Denny told me you went back to that farm today."

Denny the blabbermouth. I got some stress in case

he'd said anything he shouldn't have. "Did he say anything about Mrs. Smith? He just sort of decided she was mean, like little kids do, you know. Sometimes."

Althea looked surprised. "Just that Mrs. Smith was an old witch to you guys. I hope she wasn't too mean to you."

It was definitely time to try a diversionary tactic. I looked at all the clean people and the clean horses. "I've got to change to a jumping saddle. And maybe wash up a little bit."

She looked at her watch. "Gee, Nat. You're not going to have time to change saddles or anything else. Bill Fromm should be here any minute. But you should put your riding helmet on, at least. And your boots."

"Here, I'll swap you hair for hair. I mean hat for hat, ha-ha." Uncle Bart handed me my riding helmet. I gave him back his Buffalo Bills hat. I hoped I wasn't going to have to ask him for it every single day while I worked for the witch. Days and days and *days* of hair jokes. I'd had enough hair jokes to last me until I was about thirty-two years old.

He grinned at me. "Buckle your helmet tight and take Mindy Blue on into the ring."

I trotted Mindy Blue into the outdoor arena and joined the people circling the ring at a walk. I knew some of the students on account of they boarded their horses at Uncle Bart's. The Loomis kids, Brett and Jeff were there, and so were a couple of ladies Mom's age. Brett Loomis was this big-time brat rich kid and her brother wasn't much better. I pulled my helmet down and kept Mindy Blue away from Brett's horse Fancy. I couldn't stand it if Brett saw my hair. It was bad enough that I looked like I'd been rode hard and put away wet.

Bunkie and Belle had come back from wherever they'd spent the day. They were sitting on two fence posts. I rode over to pet them and say hi. Bunkie flattened her ears and jumped off the post when I brought Mindy Blue up to her, but good old Belle stayed right there, purring like anything. I leaned out of the saddle and whispered, "Old Peg's just fine!" and his purr got louder. "And I figured out part of the spell. It's the herbs in the square bottles she's got in the kitchen. There's just more two clues. About the noble metal and the heart's hope." I tickled Belle's ears.

"Where *is* Bill?" Brett Loomis called out in this cross way. "It's ten past two. The clinic was supposed to start promptly at two o'clock. I have a hair appointment at five."

Belle gave this little "chirrup!" and jumped off the post and ran away. Which just went to show you that he was this great cat. He didn't like loud people who thought hair appointments were as important as horses. Or hair.

Well, we circled the ring for another five minutes before Bill Fromm showed up. I would have had time to change Mindy Blue's saddle. And washed up.

When he rode into the ring, I just about *died*.

Bill Fromm was the cutest boy I'd ever seen. Except for Brian Kurlander.

He was just fabulous.

I wondered how old he was. Maybe about the age of the senior boys at school. He sat in his jumping saddle as straight and calm as anything. His hair was blond. It was cut so that he had little curls on his forehead and at the back of his neck. His eyes were this beautiful green color, like a river. He was riding Scooter. Scooter—who could be the rowdiest mare in the stables when she had a mind to—worked under him with her neck arched, her tail held high, and a light prance to her step.

Brett Loomis noticed how fabulous Bill Fromm was, too, of course.

I rubbed my neck where my hair should have been. Then I wondered how smelly I was from all that work with Old Peg. And I *really* had to talk to Mom about using maybe just a little lipstick. I'd got some, just in case.

I got so embarrassed about my hair that I slouched right down in my seat and wished I were dead. I pulled Mindy Blue behind Mrs. Rose, a perfectly nice lady with a very large horse. If I kept out of the way, Bill Fromm might not notice the saddle. Or me. Too much.

"Sorry I'm a little late."

Bill Fromm had the nicest voice!

"Collect your reins, please."

Brett Loomis took off her helmet and patted her hair. Even under the riding helmet, it was perfect. Brett always looked perfect. Except for the one time her horse Fancy dumped her in a manure pile, which I was wishing would happen again right now.

"Can we ask questions, Bill?" she cooed in this absolutely icky voice.

"Sure." He smiled. His teeth were white. His face was tanned. His hair was . . . beautiful.

Brett didn't look at me. This is a sure sign of when a person is going to be a total brat. She said, all innocent like, "I'd like you to check out my equipment. I mean, the correct attire for jumping clinics is breeches and polished boots and a white shirt. Right?"

"Right," said Bill Fromm.

"How do I look?"

"You look fine," said Bill.

"And my horse? The saddle's okay?"

"That's a Passier, isn't it? That's a wonderful saddle."

It sure is. Passiers only cost about a hundred million dollars.

"But it's all right to ride in this clinic in, say, a western saddle? And tennis shoes? I mean, I think my good friend Natalie might want to know."

"Miss Ross, is it?" Bill Fromm smiled at me. I blushed so hard I must have looked like I had a bad sunburn. "Miss Ross will be fine for this class. Next time, though, you might want to change saddles. And use boots. Okay? Collect your reins, everybody. On the bit, please."

I wanted to crawl under the nearest wagon and die like a dog. But I didn't. We Rosses aren't wimps. So I sat up straight and tipped my helmet back so that everybody could see my grubby face. I tightened my reins to get Mindy Blue on the bit. Being on the bit means that you are holding your reins very lightly, drawn tight enough so that you can feel the horse's mouth, but not tight enough so that it pulls.

We rode around in big circle, on the bit.

"Miss Loomis, you're a bit heavy on your hands. Lighten up. Lighten up. You need nice light hands like Miss Ross," said Bill Fromm.

Mindy Blue gave a little skip. Which was me, squeezing her by mistake from being happy.

The clinic went on for a while. At first it was so much fun I forgot how horrible I looked. Mindy Blue and I worked on a collected trot, then a collected canter, then figure eights. She was so good that I felt like we were flying or floating instead of being on the ground. Like Bellerophon and Pegasus, riding up Mount Olympus.

Then my life fell apart.

Once every student could do a figure eight at a collected canter, we started to go over jumps. There were six of them. Four were in a circle on the outside of the ring. Two were in the middle. To start with, you had to canter quietly in a small circle at one end of the ring, then jump the four outside jumps. When you got back to where you started, you had to turn left, go down the center of the ring and jump the two jumps in the middle. Then you had to stop.

Brett took those jumps on the outside way too fast. Then she jammed down the middle. Poor old Fancy just plain skidded to a halt and refused the first center jump. Brett's perfect makeup was all streaky with sweat and her face was red.

Hmm, I thought. And tried not to snicker.

"Again, please, Miss Loomis," said Bill Fromm.

She jammed Fancy around again, clapped her heels into the horse's side, and made Fancy take the center jumps.

Everybody applauded. Nice little claps that didn't make too much noise to make the horses nervous.

"Good," said Bill Fromm, "although you need to slow down a bit, Miss Loomis. Students? You all can tell when a horse is going to refuse. Watch the ears. Feel the horse under you. When a horse refuses, the head comes up and you can feel the hindquarters clench. The horse moves way too far off the forehand. Good riders will anticipate this. Good riders are always in control. Now, Miss Ross. If you could take Mindy Blue around for us, please?"

I cued Mindy to the canter by touching her with my outside heel, lifting the inside rein, and settling back into the saddle. We cantered in a small quiet circle. She took the four outside jumps as nice as pie. We came back to where we started. I shifted my weight in the saddle to the right and pushed with my outside leg. We turned in a nice little way and went down the center even nicer then pie.

I didn't even feel it coming.

Mindy Blue went berserk.

All of a sudden Mindy Blue screeched this high, panicked whinny. She went straight up in the air. Then she bucked. And I mean *bucked*. She bucked so hard my helmet flew off. My feet came out of the stirrups. I grabbed my right rein hard and short and pulled it down by my ankle. This turned Mindy's head so far to the right that she couldn't see where she was going. It brought her head up, so that she couldn't get her nose down around her front feet to buck some more. So now she wriggled and crow-hopped so hard that I thought my teeth were going to go right through my jaw.

Uncle Bart was right there. He grabbed Mindy's bridle and shouted "Whoa!" Althea jumped off Alternativ and was on Mindy's other side. The two of them got Mindy Blue under control.

Not me.

Uncle Bart handed me my helmet. I stuck it back on and tried like heck not to cry. I wasn't going to sob my guts out. A good rider is always in control.

Right.

I bit my lip so hard it bled. *That* made me forget about crying.

"Are you all right?" Uncle Bart asked. For once, he wasn't teasing me. "Dismount, Natalie, and take a break. I can't understand this. Mindy Blue behaving like a maniac? It's the damnedest thing I've ever seen."

I must have scared him. Uncle Bart never swears in front of us kids.

Bill Fromm rode up on Scooter. "This happens to all of us," he said, "even the best riders."

I was so far beyond embarrassment, it wasn't funny.

"I'm fine," I said. I sat up on Mindy Blue. I patted her neck. It was sweating. She rolled her eyes. She was shaking.. "Something scared her."

"I didn't see a thing," said Uncle Bart. "I mean, one minute you were loping on down the ring, then . . .

Wow. I'm just glad you weren't knocked unconscious."

Well, *I* wished I was unconscious. Everybody was looking at me. Everyone was very quiet in the way people get when there's been a major accident. I tried to act casual. I gathered the reins up and settled back on the saddle.

Bill Fromm smiled at me. "Miss Ross, maybe you'd like to take Mindy Blue out of the ring and settle her a bit. Everybody else? Let's try a collected trot."

"We'll be fine," I said. I was so humiliated I could hardly get the words out. Good horsemen don't quit. And I wasn't a quitter. I wanted to trot and walk Mindy Blue along with everybody else. So I did.

By the time four o'clock came, I was calm again, and Mindy Blue was her regular self. Bill Fromm asked us all to dismount, and we walked our horses around and around the ring until they were cooled off. Then Uncle Bart came into the arena, a box in his hands.

"I'd like to make an announcement," he said. "If all the students could come to the center of the ring, please?"

I brought Mindy Blue to the center of the ring, right next to Brett Loomis. I said hi and she said hi back in a way that made me think she wasn't going to be as much of a brat as usual. Then she said, "You cut your hair."

Like, no kidding.

"It's so *awful*," she said. "You look just like a boy."

Aaaaggh!

"People," said Uncle Bart, clapping his hands for

attention. "I have an announcement to make. Saturday, four days from now, we're going to have a little competition."

Everybody applauded.

"Saturday will be the end of the five-day clinic Bill here has run for you And I think you all agree that if today's lesson is any example, you're all going to learn a lot."

The applause was even louder this time.

"I have to say that Bill's the best rider and teacher I've come across, in all my years of being on the circuit," Uncle Bart continued. "And to celebrate that, I'm going to award the most improved student a small trophy." He waved the box in the air. "I'd like to show it to you."

He opened the box up and took out a beautiful heart trophy. "The Heart's Hope Trophy," Uncle Bart said. "For the horse and rider who demonstrate the most heart in the next four days."

I almost fell over. I barely heard Uncle Bart going on about how "heart" was a term horse people used for courage, and honesty, and well, *heart*. About how "heart" was the best measure of any horse and rider's performance. He'd keep it in the tack room so we could all see it anytime we wanted. It was made of brass and came from the trophy shop in town . . . blabber, blabber, blabber, blabber.

I was too excited to listen to it all.

That trophy was the heart's hope of the spell.

I was so excited I almost swallowed my spit. Mindy Blue and I had to win that trophy. We had to. Maybe I *could* get Denny and me out of this mess.

Except that I wouldn't get a chance to win it until Saturday. Four more days. It wouldn't take that witch that long to figure out where the "desk of Natalie Ross" was.

I had to think about this. I'd never in my life swiped so much as a pack of gum from the grocery store. But I'd never had a witch after me, either. A witch who knew my address. I had to work fast. I had to steal that trophy.

I sneaked a look around at Uncle Bart. He was talking to Bill Fromm. He didn't have the box. Which meant he'd put it in the tack room already. I hoped he and Bill weren't going to stick around too long. I could hang out until they left and then snatch the trophy.

I took Mindy Blue into the barn to sponge her off and brush her out. I hitched her to the cross ties and took my time. Finally, Denny showed up from wherever he'd been playing with Brandy. I pulled him into an empty stall in case anyone was listening. "We're almost ready, Denny. I've got everything we need to do the spell."

"Did you get the herbs?"

"The herbs? No. But I found where they are. And you saw that Heart's Hope Trophy? I'll bet you anything that's the heart's hope the spell talks about. Mindy Blue and I have to win it. Or get it. Somehow." I wasn't about to let on I was thinking of stealing and set another bad example for Denny. He'd already had one when Belle told him to take the paperweight in the first place. "And when we do, all we'll have to figure out is what a 'noble metal' is."

"You can't win that trophy," Denny said.

I looked at him. This didn't sound like Denny at all. "I can, too! It's for the most improved rider. And after today it'll be easy to be the most improved. I mean, did you see her?" I patted Mindy Blue. "She went totally bonkers. Anything'll be an improvement after that."

"Does winning that heart thing mean you have to take Mindy over that fence in the middle?" asked Denny. " 'Cause if it is, you're sunk. Torpedoed. Spiderman couldn't get Mindy over that fence. Mindy's never gonna get over that fence."

"Shut up, Denny. What do you know, anyway? You think bikes are better than horses."

"The fence turned into a lizard. A giant slimy lizard. With fire coming out of it. Just before Mindy Blue was supposed to jump."

"It did not, Dennis Ross."

"It did, too!"

"You're crazy! You didn't see any such thing. And besides. If that fence looked like a giant lizard, everyone else would have seen it, too."

"It was a huge lizard," said Denny. "A magic one. I saw it. The witch did it. She knows where to find us. And she's going to get us."

"You're kidding."

"Nope."

"Oh, boy."

"If that trophy is for the spell, I'd better swipe it."

"Denny . . ."

"Well?"

"Okay. *Okay!* But it's just this one time. Do you

understand me? And when the spell's broken, we put it right back."

"I don't want the stupid thing," said Denny.

He zipped off like he was on wheels, ducked into the tack room, then took off after a few seconds straight for home. From the way he held his stomach, I knew he'd swiped it.

I finished cleaning up Mindy Blue and went home. What a great day. Now Denny was a crook. Twice. A two-time loser. And it was all my fault.

Worst of all—the witch knew who I was.

CHAPTER

SEVEN

AT DINNER MY PARENTS DECIDED I WAS CRAZY.

Althea was there to eat with us. Denny had two of his Transformer men under his napkin and was making them from men into monster machines and back again. Once in a while he'd give me this big grin and mouth "the trophy" with his big fat mouth. At least he didn't say it aloud.

Althea didn't say much, just ate lots and lots of peas. I guess she likes them. Bunkie and Belle were sitting underneath the table. I snuck them little bits of meat loaf, which is what we were eating.

So it was quiet. Until Mom and Dad started this talk about how I needed to relax a little. That summer was a time for rest and re-cu-per-a-tion, which I found out was a word that means you can hang out instead of working.

And I found out they thought I was crazy.

Well, they didn't exactly say that I was crazy. But anytime you get speeches that start with "Natalie, we admire your independence, but . . ." and "Natalie, we want you to have some control over your own life, but . . ." I get this wriggly feeling, like: Don't you think I know that? Do you think I'm crazy?

Then I thought about Althea not saying much. Had Uncle Bart found out the Heart Hope Trophy was missing? And did they think I'd stolen it? My own parents? Of course, I had, but jeez!

So they talked about how important it is to become a woman with confidence, whatever that means, but at the same time not to "take risks." (So good ol' Uncle Bart had blabbered about Mindy Blue being spooked by the giant lizard. Of course, all he knew was that it was a fence, but jeez!) I could tell that the next thing from this woman-of-confidence stuff would be your own perfectly good mom and dad acting embarrassing and telling you about puberty and hormones. And if they went from that to how they couldn't understand how a daughter of theirs could be a sneak thief unless her hormones were really whacked, well . . . It would be so awful I would just need to change my life. And, like, move to Detroit.

Lucky for me, they switched from the woman-of-confidence stuff to being a Well-Integrated-Adult and didn't get into hormones. Or thievery. I absolutely loathe talk about hormones. And I'm *not* a crook.

"Riding gives you confidence," said Mom, "and you do a wonderful job of taking care of Denny. So we think you're doing quite enough toward becoming a Well-Integrated-Adult."

I squirmed. They didn't know about the trophy, then. They wouldn't be so proud of me taking care of Denny if they'd known I'd in-sight-ed him to steal stuff, or whatever that word is. And they wouldn't be talking Well-Integrated-Adult, either. A Well-Integrated-Adult is this person I'm supposed to be. I don't think I'm going to get there until I'm, like, forty. What a Well-Integrated-Adult does is be responsible for her little brother and keep her room clean and get good grades in geography. The Well-Integrated-Adult speech was a good sign. If they'd known about the swiped trophy, we would be talking Aberrant Behavior.

"So what we think, honey," Dad said as we started in on the strawberry shortcake, "is that you're trying to do too much at once. This job at Pegasus Farms, for example. Bart talked to Amos Barker. You know who Mr. Barker is, don't you?"

Yeah. The one who thinks it's weird for boys to be polite.

"Amos said that Mrs. Smith isn't very well liked in town. Rude with the store owners. That sort of thing. And after Althea told us how tired you looked today . . ."

I looked over at Althea, who'd taken all the whipped cream off her strawberry shortcake and given it to Denny on account of she diets. She rolled her eyes in a sort of "sorry" look. I grinned at her to let her know it was okay by me to say I was tired. I *was* tired.

". . . we think it's best you give up the job."

That got my attention.

"Mrs. Smith is a *very* rude woman," said Mom, turning pink.

"She is?" I said. "I mean, I know she is, but—" I stopped. It isn't polite to ask your mother how do *you* know? But that's what I wanted to find out.

Dad cleared his throat. "We stopped by Pegasus Farms on our way back from the our trip to Canandaigua today. While you were at the clinic. Just to see where you were working, Nat. She virtually accused you . . . well, she did accuse you and Denny of taking something from her home!"

"And," said Mom, "Mrs. Smith was perfectly horrible. About other things. So Dad and I decided that we'd pay for all of your clinic, Natalie. And it's not because we don't want to teach you the value of money. We know that you and Denny didn't take anything. You wouldn't insist on going back there if you had. It's because that Mrs. Smith is . . . well. Never mind. We don't want you to go back there. That's all." She closed her lips together, which meant she wasn't going to say another word. The only time she would say another word was if her friend Mrs. Almeter was over for coffee, and then she'd say a lot, but I'd have to go out of the room. Nobody ever tells me anything cool.

"I have to go back," I said glumly. "Because of the horse."

"The horse looks okay," said Dad carefully. "We wanted to check that out, too. The area where she's stabled it is small, of course. But it's exceptionally clean."

Of course it was! I'd practically broken my neck getting that place clean!

"And the horse is a little thin, I'll grant you that. Very thin. But its coat is well cared for. We discussed this last evening, Nat. There's good hay and grain on the premises. And the water bucket was scrubbed and filled. So the horse looks just fine. We couldn't make a case for animal abuse."

Well, Old Peg wasn't going to *stay* fine, that's for sure, if I didn't get over there every day to keep him clean and feed him. "It's like this, Mom," I said. "I like . . . ah . . . ah . . . the authority of making my own paycheck." Which was what I heard Dad say to one of their agency's clients only last month.

"You what?" said Mom.

I felt a little paw on my knee and I sneaked a look down. Marmalade-colored. So it was Belle.

"I want to go back to work?" I said to the paw.

The claws dug into my knee, just a little.

"I don't want to go back to work?" I asked.

I heard a nice big purr. Whew! That was a relief. Of course, Belle couldn't have known that I'd blown my cover, but still . . .

Then the most incredible thing happened.

Belle dropped the spell in my lap.

The witch didn't have it anymore!

Belle must have run off to Pegasus Farms and gotten it after Mindy Blue went totally insane.

But that's not what was incredible. I mean, the only way I could have missed it before was because

I was, like, stressed to the max after having worked for a witch, having my horse go berserk, dressing like a boy, and being forced into being a criminal. All in one day. What was incredible was *I knew who Belle really was!*

Jeez! I was so shocked, a big piece of strawberry shortcake fell out of my mouth.

I became aware, slowly, that there was a funny kind of silence at the table.

"Natalie?" said Mom in a worried way. "You look pale . . . oh, David! She is going through a crisis! I was right!"

I looked at Mom and Dad. Who were looking at me. So was Althea. A crisis? I knew it. They *did* think I wanted a sex-change operation. I glared at Denny. This was all his fault. Denny was oblivious, which is a word that means zoned out and not-on-this-planet. Denny is mostly oblivious unless it concerns Spider-man.

"Okay," I said,

"Okay what?" asked Dad.

"Okay that I don't go back to work for Mrs. Smith."

That made Mom relax, but it brought Denny in from outer space. "You gotta," he said. "You gotta go back."

"No, I don't, Denny."

"Yes, you *do*. You gotta get—*ow!*" He bent over and grabbed his leg under the table.

The marmalade paw was gone from my knee. I just bet it was clawing Denny's. I grinned. Served him right. It was okay for *me* to get made into witch stew, was it?

"Why don't we just have a nice quiet evening at home tonight?" said Dad in a loud voice. "Would you like to rent a videotape from Blockbuster? We can— darn!" He grabbed his leg. "What in the heck is that cat up to?"

Belle zipped out from under the table and ran to the dining-room window. He turned his big green eyes on Dad.

"Or maybe you and Althea and Denny could work on that science project for school," said Dad, very slowly.

Belle squeezed his eyes shut.

"Okay," I said. This was *so* cool. That Belle could, like, hypnotize Dad.

"Studying's *very* relaxing," said Mom, like she was about to get an argument. "And Althea makes learning so much *fun. . . .*"

I looked at my mom. I couldn't think of one single little time when Mom could get hypnotized. Maybe this was part of the difference between boys and girls. "I said it's fine, Mom. We'll start right after supper."

Belle rolled himself into a snug little ball and purred. Bunkie sat right next to him and washed his ears, which he didn't mind a bit.

After dinner I went to my room to get my project book for tutoring. Denny followed me. He slammed the door behind him, dropped onto my rug, and wriggled under the bed.

"Denny."

No answer.

"Denny! Come out of there."

He shoved himself back out. The Pegasus paper-weight was in one hand.

"What are you *doing*?"

"If you're not gonna help get Pegasus out, I'll do it!"

"Denny, of course I'm going to help Pegasus out. That's what all this is about!"

"You're not going back there. You said so! She's won! It's Witch one, Kids zero."

"You saw what happened today! She turned that fence into a lizard. She spooked Mindy Blue so much that poor horse may never jump again! You think I'm going to take that lying down? When she could have wrecked my horse for life?"

This is true. You can spook a horse so much that it won't do what it was doing when it was spooked, ever again. It's because of the way horses remember stuff, which is different from us humans. If they've been scared just once, they think: *Fence monster!* every time they see a perfectly good fence. Althea says this is why horses have been around this world for a million years. They didn't have to get eaten by a Siberian tiger more than once to know to stay away from danger.

"So?" Denny demanded.

"So of course I'm not giving up. You're supposed to be the wizard, right? And you don't know what's going on?"

There was a *skritch-skritch-skritch* at my bedroom door.

"I know what's going on," Denny said. Ha. He looked as clueless a seven-year-old can look.

Skritch-skritch-skritch.

"Then who's at that door?" I said.

Denny's eyes got big. "The *witch!*" he yelled.

I clapped my hand over his mouth. It was sticky from the strawberries. "It's not Mrs. Smith! Okay?"

He nodded.

I took my hand away, walked over to the door, and opened it.

Belle walked in, of course.

"Mr. Dennis Ross," I said. "Meet Belle. Otherwise known as Bellerophon. Rider of Pegasus. The boy who shaved off the beards of the gods. Which was," I said, looking at Bellerophon rolling around at my feet, "what started this whole thing in the first place. Do you know how much poetry would be around if you hadn't gone where you shouldn't't've?"

"Cool!" said Denny.

Because of course I'd figured it out. A witch who'd given a horse like Pegasus a girl's name would do it to a cat, too. Belle was Bellerophon. I couldn't believe I hadn't gotten it way before this.

I picked Belle up and cuddled him. His big green eyes looked into mine. "Who's a cute kitty?" I said, tickling him. "Oh, who's a cute, cute kitty?"

Belle stopped purring. And looked—I don't know— kinda annoyed. Cats have their dignity, Dad always says.

I dropped him to the floor with a thud. "Belle sneaked in the witch's house and brought the spell back. Now the only thing we have left to discover is what a noble metal is. And once we know that—"

"Hi, guys," said Althea, walking in.

Denny stuffed the paperweight under his T-shirt. It made him look like a short version of Normie Fassbinder, the fattest kid in school.

"You ready to go over some physics?"

Like, now? When we were just about to break the spell? With Belle's help?

"Well . . ." I started to say.

Belle went, "Meow."

"Yeah," I said. "Sure."

"We could start with noble metals, if you like. I heard you mention them when I walked in. Sorry. I didn't mean to eavesdrop. But noble metals are so interesting. And you can learn a lot about thermodynamics when discussing their characteristics."

At last! The final part of the spell!

CHAPTER

eight

THE THREE OF US SETTLED AROUND THE ROOM. I SAT propped up at the head of my bed. Althea sat cross-legged at the foot. Denny sat in the swivel chair at my desk. He likes to whirl it, bang his feet, and make noise. Normally, I yell at him, but this wasn't a normal time.

"Where did you hear about noble metals?" Althea asked.

How much could I tell Althea?

Now, Althea had been smack in the middle of our first adventure when Denny turned our aunt Matty into a griffin. So had Aunt Matty herself, of course. After that adventure was all over, neither one of them remembered a *thing* about the griffin. Did this mean that I could tell Althea about the spell now? That'd she'd be able to help us again and then forget about it? Or was the forgetting a onetime thing like a start-up part of the magic? If she didn't forget this time, I'd be in the soup for sure. All the adults in my life were sure I was having this Crisis. That I wanted to be a boy instead of a girl.

I looked at Belle. He purred.

"Did you *read* about noble metals?" said Althea, who admits that she is a curious person.

I stared at my knees, thinking about how much I could say. Then Belle hopped onto my bed and patted my arm.

His big green eyes opened and closed. Belle'd steered us right so far. He must mean for me to give Althea the spell.

"It's this ol' poem I found." I dug the spell out of my pocket. It was crumpled up. There were tooth marks in it from Belle carrying it the three miles from the witch's house.

"A poem? There's not much poetry left in this world, that's for sure," Althea said.

I winked at Belle. He winked back. Althea smoothed the spell on the bedspread and read aloud.

First Noble Metals encircle the glass,
Then Herbs must set fire
To Heart's Hope from your past.
As Time speeds on forward
The glass melts and flows.
And the Wise Poet's freed
as the wind's free
to go.

"How odd," said Althea. "I mean, it's interesting. But this is your handwriting, Natalie. You couldn't have . . . I mean, did you write this?"

And here I'd been having this whole adventure without having to tell one fib! I mean, I'd had to steal, yeah. But no fibs.

"Well, sort of." I picked at a spot of strawberry shortcake on my jeans. "I guess. I kind of heard it around, about all that stuff."

"Gosh. This could even tie in to our physics lesson tonight. I didn't think my physics lessons were having that much effect." Althea frowned. "Hmm. This reminds me . . . this reminds me. . . ."

Did she remember about the griffin after all? I held my breath.

"Well." She shook her head, like Mindy Blue does when she's got flies in her ears. Her long red hair flew around her face. Just like Mindy's mane. She poked her big round glasses up her nose. "Where did you hear that glass is a liquid? I don't remember telling you that."

"Glass is a liquid?"

"Sure. At least, old-time glass is a liquid. Before glassblowers knew enough to put additives in it, like lead. You remember when your mom and dad and the three of us went to Monticello last year? And saw Jefferson's home?"

Denny and I'd been dragged on this historical tour of some dead president's house. He'd lived a long time ago in a house called Monticello that was a couple hundred years old.

"And you recall the windows in the house? How

the glass in them was distorted? Sort of bubbly and bumpy? Well, that's because the windows are melting."

Excuse me? Melting glass?

"You remember about molecules," Althea said.

"Yeah. All the stuff in the world is called matter. Everything is made of matter. Matter is made of molecules. Molecules are little specks of atoms and quarks all stuck together in a little ball shape. Then these ball shapes are attached to each other by little rods. That's how Denny's mag—" I stopped. Like I said before, Denny's a nano-magician. A nano-magician can move these little rods from one molecule to another, so that stuff—I mean matter—is shaped into something else. And I'd just been about to tell Althea that Denny's magic could do this!

"Right. Molecules that make up inorganic materials like minerals are in the shape of crystals. These crystal minerals are called compounds. Sand is an example. Sand is a stable compound. A stable compound means that the molecules of crystals are evenly arranged next to each other. They have plane surfaces. The stuff that makes up glass is sand, essentially. Glass is made by heating sand up until it becomes a liquid solid. Then you shape the liquid solid into whatever you want. Windows, paperweights, whatever. Got that?"

I said I guessed so.

"So you heat the sand, and these crystals melt. You cool the melted sand off so fast that the crystals don't re-form. And then you've got a compound which doesn't bind to itself. It's not stable. The surfaces of the molecules are no longer evenly arranged.

"Now, you remember those laws of thermodynamics?"

"Yeah," Denny said. "They're cool."

I remembered them, too. It's what got me to understand about Denny's magic. The first law is:

Stuff starts out all neat and tidy. It moves all the time.

The second law is:

Stuff keeps on *moving toward being a big mess.*

The third law is:

This moving stuff always *goes from neat and tidy to a big mess.* (It never goes back to neat and tidy.)

The Fourth Law is:

Stuff always has temperature. It's either always hot or always cold. There's never *no temperature at all*!

"Right!" said Althea. "Now, what happens when you apply the laws to glass? Remember, stuff always keeps on moving toward chaos. That is, a 'big mess.'"

"It melts?" I said

"Well. Dissolution would be a good word. Moving toward a similar chaotic state would be a good phrase. But yeah, let's use 'melts.' Now we're talking

about 'melting' over *thousands* of years, here. But in
thousands and thousands of years all the glass at
Monticello will be 'melted' right off the windows and
onto the ground. If the place is still there after
thousands of years, of course."

Thousands of years. When Denny unmagicked the
griffin, he'd had to unbake the cake of Aunt Matty,
his parakeet, and my good ol' cat Bunkie by pushing
time backward. Now it looked like he'd have to speed
up the melting of that paperweight by pushing time
forward. The way Denny pushed time forward was
to use that fourth law of thermodynamics and make
things have no-temperature. When things have no-
temperature at all, the molecules and atoms and
quarks don't move. Then Denny uses his magic to
make the molecules move. He can push them backward, to make time reverse. I hoped he could push
them forward, to make time speed up. I wondered
how fast he'd have to push time forward to make the
glass in the paperweight melt in like, a couple of
minutes.

"So wherever you got the idea for this poem, Natalie, you were right. About time and liquid glass."

"I just . . . heard it around," I repeated.

"You 'heard it around' about noble metals, too?
There's only two of them, you know. Gold and platinum."

"A noble metal is gold?"

"Yes. Gold and platinum are some of the sub-
stances in the world that are not affected by the laws
about change. They don't decay. They don't oxidize.
They don't break down. They're what we call stable,

that is, they can't break down to anything more than they are. They've already 'melted' to the max, if you like. They are not affected by the passage of time, the way that glass is, for example, or most other matter." Althea read the spell again. Belle's purr was so loud you probably could have heard it on the moon. "Now, if this were a spell, instead of a poem," Althea said in a dreamy kind of voice ("Purr, *purr*, PURRRR," went Belle), "and if you were going to speed the 'melting' of the glass, you'd have to surround the glass with gold. Or platinum, so that the reaction wouldn't spread."

Belle yawned, suddenly. Then, like cats do, he fell asleep. Hypnotizing must be hard work.

Althea blinked, just like she'd been a little asleep, too. "Anyway. Nice poem, Natalie. Now. Let's get to work. Nat, why don't you boot up your computer, and we'll check out the project specifications."

This project we were working on was for a special science class in school. Some guy named Charles Babbage about a hundred years ago actually made a computer before computers were invented! It was this big huge machine that had about a zillion metal parts that were all the same. Some of us kids at school were making a little bitty model of it. Anyhow, I had the drawing of the model on my Apple computer. I shoved Denny off my desk chair, sat down, and booted up.

Suddenly Belle howled. I jumped about a foot. I spun around in my chair. Belle was sitting up on the bed, his fur puffed out like a huge sticker burr. *"Aaaaoooooooohhhh!"* howled Belle. He was seeing something we couldn't see. My skin crawled. The room was suddenly cold.

"Wow!" said Denny.

"Good grief," said Althea. "That poor thing. What do you suppose is wrong? Is he sick?"

Belle glared wildly at the air. Then he streaked under the bed like all the dogs in Cayuga Lake were after him. Denny scrambled down on his knees and crawled in after him. After a few seconds he came back out. "Belle wants to stay in there, Natalie."

"Well, let him."

Just then, I heard the phone ring from the living room. Then Dad's voice: "Althea! There's a call for you!"

"Excuse me, guys. Natalie, why don't you call up the encyclopedia and look up noble metals? It might have a better explanation than I gave you." She rushed out of the room. Althea didn't have a boyfriend as far as I knew, but from the look on her face . . . well, you never know about tutors.

I input the command for the encyclopedia into my Apple. When the picture and music came on for the index, I keyed in *herbs*.

"What're you doing?" asked Denny, breathing down my neck.

"I'm going to find out if there's someplace we can go to get the herbs to make the spell work. Remember? 'Then Herbs must set fire to Heart's Hope from your past?' I don't want to go back to Pegasus Farm. I can't go back there, now that she's found out Brian Kurlander is really Natalie Ross. So if there are herbs, like, growing in people's gardens, the encyclopedia will have a picture. Then we can go out and look in the woods or whatever."

NO LISTING FOR HORSE-BANE, the screen read.

"Dang, Denny. The first one I found isn't in the encyclopedia."

"What about the others?" said Denny.

I input. The screen said:

NO LISTING FOR HORSE-WOUND
NO LISTING FOR FORSE-WORT
NO LISTING FOR HORSE-NIP

The screen saver came on all of a sudden. I banged the delete key, the option-quit keys, and a whole bunch of other keys. For one thing, I hadn't exited the encyclopedia file, so the darn screen saver shouldn't have been up there. For another, *I* sure'd never downloaded *that* screen saver into my computer. It was all kinds of ugly swirly colors. Black and white and red, mostly. They swirled and swirled . . .

. . . *and Zeuxippe Smith stared at us from the screen!*

She didn't even look partway human now. Her smooth round face was like a doll mask. Her red, red eyes glittered. She turned, turned on the screen, those wild red eyes searching.

Childrennnn, she said hissing. *Nisssee ssstrong childrennn.*

Flames leaped up from behind her. She began to spin. Faster. Faster. And as she spun, the blobby red-

and-black screen merged into a whirl of vomit-colored specks.

The whirling slowed, like a top losing spin. Zeuxippe Smith's face dissolved ... changed ... morphed. ...

A giant snake reared and hissed at us! Its tongue forked and flickered, now to the left, and with a hiss, it said, *Where?*

Now to the right, hissing: *Where?*

And then, in a horribly human, right-there-in-the-room-with-us voice: "THERE!"

Straight at us!

"Duck, Denny!"

The two of us dived under the bed.

It'd been a long time since I'd crawled under a bed. It was a tight fit. Denny managed just fine, as, of course, had Belle. But I had to keep my face turned to one side. My left ear was mashed against the carpet so hard I couldn't hear. The cloth part of the box springs scraped my right cheek.

A whirling, smashing tornado filled the room. Belle stuck his nose out from under the dust ruffle and growled like a tiger. I grabbed Denny. I reached for Belle. His growls were ferocious. His entire body shook. I thought the noise inside in my room would never stop. I opened my mouth to yell. The whirlwind snatched my voice away. The room spun and flickered with bolts of sickly green-yellow light. I shut my eyes and held my hand over Denny's eyes.

The whirlwind died.

The hissing stopped.

I opened my eyes slowly, afraid of what I'd see.

A pair of feet walked by. Tennis shoes, with scrunched-down white socks.

"Guys?" said Althea. "Where are you?" She squatted down. "What are you all doing under the bed?"

I took a breath. Then another one.

Denny wriggled and squirmed. "Leggo!"

"Just . . . um . . . trying to get Belle out." I said. "There's . . . ah . . . something funny with my Apple. Do you see anything weird?"

Althea straightened up, so all I saw was her tennis shoes again. "What's wrong with it?"

"The screen went all wonky. It was, like, gruesome."

"Well, it's not gruesome now." I heard the *tap-tap-tap* of the keyboard. "It's crashed, that's what it's done. It's frozen. What the heck did you guys do to it?"

"There's no gross and disgusting picture on it? Of, say, a really ugly face? Or a snake? Do you see any snakes?"

"No, Natalie. No snakes. The little Macintosh frown icon's on. I told you, it looks like a system crash." Her face came into view, upside down. "Don't you want to come out of there?"

I looked at Belle. He was crouched down on all four feet. His tail twitched back and forth a little, but except for that, he looked normal. As much as a boy who's been turned into a cat can look normal.

"Sure. C'mon, Denny."

We crawled out. I took a fast glance at the screen. It was totally gray except for this sad little Macintosh face. "Dang," I said.

Althea tapped at the keyboard again. "Is your system backed up?"

I took a second to figure this out. We'd just started using computers at school, and they were cool but confusing.

"You should have all the stuff that's stored on your computer backed up on floppy disks," said Althea.

"She's got 'em," said Denny, who thinks it's hilarious that a seven-year-old kid knows more about computers than me. "They're here." He pulled open the big drawer at the side of my desk and dumped out about forty floppy disks packed in a big box. "You got to reinstall 'em, Natalie."

"You mean load each one of those floppies? It'll take hours!"

"Well, your system's bombed," said Denny gleefully. "The witch bombed it."

I kicked him to shut up. "Who was on the phone, Althea?" I said as a diversionary tactic.

"Oh. Um." Her face turned pink. "Well, it was Bart. Actually. You know, your uncle Bart."

"What'd he want? Did he want to know where my hair was? Or maybe he's found my hair and wants to give it me? Or maybe he bought a wig?"

"No. No. No. Nothing like that." Althea put her glasses on. Then she took them off. Then she put them on again. "He wants to go to the movies."

Well!

"I don't want to go to the movies," said Denny.

I poked him. "Shut up, Denny."

"Well, I don't! I got stuff to do."

"Denny, *you* aren't invited to the movies."

"Althea just said—"

"Althea said Uncle Bart called to ask *her* to the movies." I was feeling better and better about Denny knowing more about computers than me. *I* knew about life. Ha! I patted Althea's arm. "You go on to the movies, Althea. We can't work on the mechanical-computer project anyhow until Denny reloads my hard drive. You want to borrow some lipstick or something?"

"Do I need lipstick?" She patted her mouth. "Natalie! You're not supposed to have lipstick."

"It's not *mine*!" Jeez! "I'm just saving it. Here. It's pink. You can use all you want." I scrabbled in my drawer and dug it from where I kept it under Brian Kurlander's letters. "There. You go have a good time."

"Thanks. If you guys are sure?"

"No problem."

"I'll see you both tomorrow."

"No problem."

"And thanks for the lipstick."

"Right."

As soon as Althea walked out of the bedroom, I slammed the door shut and went to my closet.

"What are you doing?" Denny said.

"Never mind. You go play with your Spiderman stuff." I found a jacket and put it on.

"What are you doing?"

"Denny." I crouched down and looked at him. Right into his beady little blue eyes. "You know she's found us."

"The witch." His freckles stood out.

"Yep." I tried to act cool, because I didn't want him to know how scared I was. "I think it was because of those herbs I was looking for. They're magic herbs. Not listed in the encyclopedia. Or anywhere else on this earth. When I put them all together like that, I think they made a sort of spell. A spell that called her. So she knows for sure it's us—me, actually— that knows the spell that will melt the paperweight. So I've got to get those herbs right now, Denny. We have to break that spell tonight! And I've got to sneak into her kitchen, snatch the herbs, and sneak out again. Here. Give me the paperweight."

"I'm coming, too."

"No, you're not. You stay here and be with Belle. He might have more messages to send us."

"Uh-uh. I'm coming, too."

"You can't, Denny. It's too dangerous. I have to swipe those bottles of herbs from the kitchen, take the whole mess out to the shed, and then light a fire. If she finds you, she'll . . ." Turn him into a pig, I thought. But I didn't want to say it.

Belle crawled out from under the bed. He walked up to Denny, sat down, and stared at him with his big green eyes.

"See? Belle agrees with me. I have to go," said Denny. He took his Spiderman yo-yo out of his pocket and gave it a spin. Trying to act cool like the big boys. He gave me a big freckled grin. "I'm the magician, remember?"

CHAPTER

nine

DENNY WAS RIGHT. WE BOTH HAD TO GO. WE BOTH had to be there to break the spell.

I went to my bedroom door. Stuck my head out into the hall. It was dark and quiet. Mom and Dad must have gone to bed early. I came back. Denny and Belle were waiting. I picked up the Pegasus paperweight, the spell, and the Heart's Hope Trophy and slung them into my backpack. I had a souvenir pack of matches on my bureau from a restaurant where Mom and Dad had taken us to eat. I put those in my jeans. I had to have something to light the herbs.

I made sure the pearl necklace was around my neck, then touched Brian's charm bracelet for luck.

"Okay," I said, "we're ready."

Belle yowled. Despite the heat of a late-June night in Cayuga Lake, I shivered.

We tiptoed out of the house and got our bikes. It was scary, pedaling uphill in the dark. The moon was huge and white. The sky was filled with stars.

The three miles went a lot faster at night. We stopped at the beginning of the driveway. The Pegasus Farms sign sagged at the end. The moon was so full I could read the sign. It was the same as the ad we'd seen in the supermarket.

STABLE HAND WANTED
PEGASUS FARMS
ZEUXIPPE SMITH, OWNER
ONE CORY CORNERS ROAD

The little flying horse that had been drawn in the corner was all alone. Its wings were droopy and sad.

We walked the bikes on the grass so as not to make any noise. My heart was thumping away like a trapped pigeon. The shed loomed up in the dark. Belle made a small "chiruping" sound. Old Peg blew back with a whicker so low I could barely hear it.

We walked past the shed. The house seemed to sulk in the pine trees. The pointed peak looked like claws, reaching to the moonlit sky.

"Remember," I whispered in Denny's ear, "we go quietly up to the back window. I lift you up. You open the window. Reach in. The horse herbs are just underneath, on the right." I thought a second. I'd been facing the window from the inside of the kitchen when I'd seen them. Denny would be coming in the other way, so it would be backward. "Nope. Not on the right. Get the ones on the left. Okay? They're in square bottles. Not like the other ones. The regular ones are round. Then we go to the shed. And *not one word* once we get close to the house, or we'll be fried apples for sure. Got it?"

"Got it."

We ditched the bikes behind some scraggly bushes. There was no sound at all as we crept up to the house. No frogs burping. No night birds. Even the wind had died, so that you could hear your own breathing. Belle padded alongside us like a ghost.

The house was as dark as the sky. I grabbed Denny's shoulder with a warning squeeze. I held my breath and listened and listened. Nothing. No noise. And no lights in any part of that scary place.

We crept around to the back. I hoisted Denny up. He opened the kitchen window with the barest *creak*. We both froze like Popsicles. Denny wriggled. He was heavy. My muscles were getting wobbly. I gritted my teeth. "Okay?"

I could feel Denny reach in.

"Got them?"

"Round ones?" Denny said in a normal voice.

"Shh!"

"Sorry. I forgot. Square ones, right?"

If that was a whisper, then I was a Chinaman, as my grandfather used to say.

"Yes. But, *quiet!*"

Denny hitched forward. Something crashed to the floor inside.

I was so scared I choked on my spit. I waited, holding my breath.

Nothing moved in the silence.

Denny wriggled again, a signal to back up. I set him on the ground. He had four bottles. I read them by the light of the moon: Horse-wound, Horse-bane, Horse-nip, Horse-wort. I hugged him with the hand that wasn't holding the bottles.

We waited a second under the eaves of the back porch, almost too scared to move. Belle brushed against my legs, his tail up and quivering. I could almost feel him say, "Come on!" We headed back to the shed. Old Peg greeted us with an eager whicker. I whispered frantically, "Quiet, boy. Quiet!" And it must have been more magic because he quieted right down. All he did was stand by the latched gate and wait while we came in. His head was high and eager.

The moonlight shone around Old Peg like a bride's veil. In the harsh sunshine, you could see his sad ribs and his shadowed eyes. In the soft light of the moon, I could see how he'd look when we freed him. When we gave him back his wings.

I crouched on the ground and took the paperweight from the backpack. It glowed like the stars. I looked at the gold horse inside, then at Old Peg, and back again. The bound spirit and his great earthly body stood exactly the same. Waiting for us to free them and make them one.

I pulled the stopper from the herb bottles and sprinkled the herbs on the ground, mixing them all up. Denny took the paperweight and put it gently in the middle.

"First Noble Metals encircle the glass," I said softly.

And stopped. The trophy sat there. A solid heart. Not gold, but brass.

How could I have been so stupid? That trophy wouldn't work!

Then Herbs must set fire to Heart's Hope from your past . . . .

I pulled at my charm bracelet, trying to think. Looked down at Brian Kurlander's heart charm.

No.

Not that.

I'd have to burn the most important thing I'd ever owned.

"What's wrong?" whispered Denny.

I reached up and patted Old Peg. I felt the scars on his shoulders, his skinny ribs under my hand. I swallowed hard. "I guess we have to burn my heart charm with the herbs. It's gold. It's a noble metal. And it's from my past. This trophy I thought would work? It won't. I was dumb, Denny. It's made of brass. Brass isn't a noble metal."

Denny isn't a bozo all the time. He just patted my arm and didn't say anything. Which was cool. I swallowed again, just to give myself a minute. I took off the bracelet. I arranged it into a perfect circle. The paperweight lay in the middle, the herbs underneath it, the gold bracelet surrounding it. The gold heart charm caught the moonlight. It looked powerful and mighty as it sat there.

"Okay, Denny. Are you ready? Do you know what to do? You have to see the paperweight as little specks. Then you make the specks stop moving. You turn them to no-temperature. Then you push the specks forward. And push fast."

"Okay."

I put one hand on the pearl necklace. "Imagine," I said to Denny, "Imagine the specks."

He bent over the paperweight. You couldn't see his freckles under the moon. The tips of his fingers began to glow with the green light of magic.

Belle growled, low and ugly.

"So," said Zeuxippe Smith from behind me. Like she was about to eat something good.

Denny shrieked. I whirled. She loomed in the dark like a terrible dream, her eyes red with the fire of her hate. Her smooth smooth hands reached out and grabbed my shoulders. Her hands were as cold as death.

"Pigs!" she screamed. "I shall turn you all into *pigs!"*

Old Peg whinnied like a great bronze trumpet. The stars seemed to shake in the sky. Old Peg ran between me and the witch, pawing and snorting. Zeuxippe darted away from his huge hooves. She raised her arms to the sky. A single flash of lightning tore across the night.

I twisted away, my hands fumbling with the matches. My hands were shaking so hard I couldn't strike them. I knew, I *knew* when her hands came down, a terrible spell would be thrown at Denny. At me. I had to light those herbs. And I had to stop her. I knew I couldn't do both.

"Web up!" screamed Denny, and that stupid Spiderman yo-yo came spinning out of the dark. It wrapped around the witch's leg. The witch's arms pinwheeled. She fell back. Belle leaped onto the witch's chest, spitting and howling. She grabbed at Belle. She held him high. She shook him and shook him. He yowled and spat, his claws raking her face. She grabbed him by the throat and squeezed.

"No!" I shouted. "Belle!"

She hoisted herself up on one arm and threw that poor cat against the fence. He bounced off and lay still. So still. I screamed, madder than I've ever been in my life.

Denny's green magic leaped through the air. It spun around the witch's head in a fiery blaze, snapping and cracking. The witch howled like a dog. She turned over and slithered on her stomach, out of the magic light.

I scrambled up. I picked up Belle's body. I was crying, I think. But I was so mad, I couldn't tell. I scraped at the matches, hugging Belle close. No breath in him. I knew that. He was dead. I knew it like you know about things you love. I scraped at the matches. I scraped and scraped.

They caught fire!

I threw the matches at the herbs, yelling *"Denny!"* as they arced through the air. He spun around fast. Held out his hands. Green fire leaped from his fingers. I held the pearl necklace and clutched Belle's body to me with the other. The matches landed on the herbs . . . smoldered . . .

. . . and burst into a great white light.

"Natalie," Denny said, in a quiet sort of way. "Put Belle in the light."

I sobbed. Gulped. Nodded. I knelt in front of the
magic fire. Put Belle's body in the light. As my hands
passed through it I could see my own bones. I shud-
dered, and laid him gently down. I backed away and
stood there. The white light was a beacon, a pillar. I
couldn't see Belle's body at all.

"Push, Denny, push!"

His hands flew wide. The green magic blazed. He
leaned into the pillar of fire.

Denny pushed.

And he pushed time forward.

The green light hit the white. You would have
thought a bomb had hit. The paperweight flared up,
flowed . . . and *melted* with a sound like forty thun-
derstorms at once.

The gold horse sprang from the melted glass. And
the gold horse flew, diamond wings bathed in a
shower of brilliance from the white, white light
around it. Up, up, and up, the gold horse flew, circling the paddock. With each circle, the gold horse
grew bigger. Thinned. Became transparent. Until it
floated like a thin horse-shaped cloak over Old Peg's
head. The veil was a sparkling net of gold cradled by
the beam of white light.

The green fire from Denny's hands flickered and
went out.

Zeuxippe Smith leaped out of the darkness. She
was changing, right before my eyes. Half snake, half
woman-shaped witch, she writhed and screamed in
rage. She yelled in spite. She beat the ground with
her fists and cursed something awful. Terrible
curses, in a language I didn't know. She crawled to-

ward the pillar. The light beat her back. The light was so white, it seemed like the moon'd come down. She cringed, her hands over her eyes, and screamed again, as if she'd been stabbed.

The gold cloak floated like water, transparent, gleaming. There was a sound like chiming bells. The cloak dropped. Swirled itself around Old Peg's head. It flowed down his neck and withers in a gentle wave, folding around his old gray coat with shimmering, quivering light.

He whinnied. A huge glad cry that shook the stars. A "welcome" cry. His body glowed like a rising moon. His wings unfolded with a sound like water racing over a wide and glorious river.

Old Peg became Pegasus. Pegasus the Flier. Pegasus the Free. He flew around the sky in a great circle, his wings beating the air. A scent like flowers came, and then . . .

. . . a voice. And it spoke: not in the way you usually hear things, but in our heads. I grabbed Denny's hand. The Voice of the Poetry of Pegasus flew with him in a stream of light from the moon.

> Star's light falls on still meadows.
> Dawn's fire catches the sun's shadow.
> Heaven's winds heal the splintered heart.
> I am Pegasus! I am free!

We watched. I think I cried. We watched as he flew, up and up and up, the shimmer of his golden body becoming one with the stars.

The white light ebbed away, like water flowing. It was like the moon returned to the sky

It was quiet. Dark.

Then the witch came back.

"Piiigs!" hissed its low and ugly voice. "Piiigs." She came at us out of the dark. The last of her human self had dropped away. She was a snake. A giant snake. Her bone-gray fangs dripped poison. Her flame-red eyes dripped hate. Her snake's head swayed. Back and forth. Back and forth. A slow whipping. An eerie rythmn.

I felt myself move. Back and forth. Back and forth. In time with the snake. In time with the snake. Denny moved with me. Side by side. We moved. . . .

She was hypnotizing Denny! "You *stop!*" I screamed.

The black eyes flared with red red hate. She uncoiled like a spring, and struck. I ducked. She missed. I grabbed Denny's hand. There was a *whoosh!* behind her. And a sound like a sword whistling through the air.

Someone hollered, "Run! Run for the bikes!"

I knew that voice! I knew it!

Belle!

We ran, Denny and me. Stumbling through the dark. Falling over stones. Tripping in holes. We fell, and got up. We fell and got up. Behind us, there was the sound of a fight. A hissing, writhing, screeching fight. And the voice that had told us to run yelled "Run!" once more. We ran faster and faster. We ran for our lives.

We got to the bikes. A giant arm slammed around

my middle. I smelled a cold cold reptile smell. I kicked out and yelled for Denny to "Go! *Go!* Go!"

A huge wind rose around us, whipping my hair in my eyes. I couldn't see! I couldn't see Denny! But I could feel the witch!

The giant arm tightened. Tightened. I could barely breathe!

There was a shout! Denny!

Denny screamed, "Let her *go!*"

A *hissssss* like steam. The giant arm dropped away.

Did she have him? Did she have my brother?

Hands grabbed at my stomach. I tried to scream, but no scream came. There was a gentle breath on my face. A satiny coat between my knees. I opened my eyes and looked down. Two freckled hands clutched my middle.

Denny!

He was sitting behind me on the back of the great flying horse!

Soft feathery wings rose and fell on either side of us. Like being brushed with clouds. The wings beat the air with gentle strokes. Faster. Faster. Higher. Higher. Until we reached the sky.

We overlooked Pegasus Farms. The lights of Cayuga Lake twinkled below us. Beyond, I could see the great span of Lake Ontario. The perfumed wings of Pegasus rose and fell around us. The winds rushed past our faces and tickled our cheeks.

Far below us, a high, sweet whistling came. There were no words, but I knew that whistle. I knew the music in it. It was a "come home!" call.

And the great horse listened. I felt the shift in his rhythm, the supple bend in his sides. He circled, lower, lower, lower, and we landed with a gentle four-beat bump as each powerful leg hit the ground.

We were back at the farm, near the shed.

The night was still, again. The herb fire flickered and danced, throwing light now here, now there. A huge mottled snakeskin was crumpled in a corner of the paddock, flung on the ground like a coat you don't like.

The witch was gone.

Pegasus folded his wings. They cupped around our legs, as soft as a bird's touch, as if a mist were real.

Footsteps came from the darkness. Pegasus whinnied, an "I'm here" call.

And Bill Fromm stepped into the circle of firelight.

His eyes were sea green. Like Belle's. His hair was marmalade gold, curled around his neck and forehead in soft curves. He wore clothes I'd only seen in books. A white tunic, pulled up on one shoulder and pinned with a gold horse's head, with ruby eyes. The other shoulder was bare.

"You were Belle," I said.

"Oh, yes."

"And Bill, too."

"And yes again. My dearest dear." Bellerophon smiled. His sea-green eyes crinkled at the corners.

His fingers touched the back of my neck, where my hair had been. And the place on my wrist where the bracelet had been.

"Let's ride," said Bellerophon.

And he leaped to Old Peg's back, holding both Denny and me in front of him.

The muscles under the winged horse's coat had not forgotten. Earthbound for so long, he now flew free. He flew like a great, bursting song. And we flew with him, Denny and Bellerophon and me. We laughed as the stars spun by. The ground below us rolled like a carpet spangled with the lights of streets and houses. We turned and swirled in circles and spirals. We glided along, the four of us, as though the air were ocean.

We flew on and on and on. Until the stars slid home. Until the moon set and the dark of deepest night began to lift.

Then dawn came. Spreading like cream in coffee. At the edge of the world, a mountain rose. Its snowy top held the butter yellow of sunshine. Velvet-green pastures cloaked its sides.

"Olympus," said Bellerophon. Then: "Children of men. Turn to me." Denny and I wriggled around on Pegasus' back. Bellerophon looked at us with his sea-green eyes. "We are home, Pegasus and I. Our thanks to you, children of men."

"The poetry," I said. My voice sounded shy. "What about the poetry? Will it come back?"

He smiled. A smile like a flower opening. "If you listen," he said. "It's always been there. For those who listen."

"Phuut!" Denny went, like the bozo he is.

"You have our thanks, wizard, my horse and me. And you, Natalie. You have my blessing."

There was a light touch on my wrist.

And they were gone.

CHAPTER

ᴛᴇɴ

I WOKE UP WITH THE SUNSHINE STREAMING THROUGH my window and Denny at my door.

"Mom says breakfast is ready *now*," he said. My cat Bunkie sat at his feet. She looked cross. This was because Denny's parakeet T.E. sat on her head.

"Get that bird off my cat, Dennis Ross."

He chirped at T.E. and held out his finger. Bunkie came and sat on my bed and started to purr her breakfast purr. I tickled her ears. I could hear Uncle Bart hollering "good morning" to somebody outside my open window. Mindy Blue would be coming in for breakfast, along with the rest of the horses. I could ride today, however far I wanted.

There'd be nothing left of the witch's place now but weedy scrubby pastures. And a burned spot where the magic fire had been.

And Pegasus was home.

I hustled out of the bathroom and to the breakfast table still half-asleep. Oatmeal this morning, with brown sugar. I looked over at Denny. He liked oatmeal. Not to eat. To splat against the ceiling with his spoon when Mom and Dad weren't looking. I was starved. I reached out for the sugar, and Dad said, "Hey, kiddo."

"Hey, Dad."

"No. I mean what happened to your heart charm? And where did you get that?"

I blinked away the sleep and looked. My charm bracelet was there.

Just like always!

The heart charm was gone. Burned in the magic fire. In its place was a diamond-winged horse looking up at me with loving ruby eyes.

The blessing.

"Oh." I smiled. "It's kind of from our work for Zeuxippe Smith. You know. For cleaning up and all."

"Saw Bart this morning. Seems Mrs. Smith's up and left town," said Dad. "Good riddance, I say. And there's some disappointing news, Natalie. Bill Fromm's left town, too. Told Bart he'd been called home. So there won't be a jumping clinic today. Bart's going to try and find another trainer."

"I haven't seen that marmalade cat around," said Mom. "Mrs. Smith treated it so badly, I can't imagine where it went."

"Belle found a nice home," said Denny. "Better than with that ol' witch."

"Denny," said Mom, in this let's-be-nice tone of voice.

"Belle went with Bill," Denny insisted.

"You don't know that, young man," said Dad.

I grinned at Denny. "It's true, I bet. Belle's got a lot better home with Bill than with that ol' witch," I said. "Sorry, Mom, but she *was*."

"You two know something you're not telling us?" Dad said in a ho-ho-ho sort of way.

"Do you believe in witches, Dad?"

"Of course not, honey. They're creatures made up from the mind of man. They're a way to explain away behaviors people don't understand. I hope you two don't believe in witches."

"Sure we do," said Denny. "That Zeuxippe Smith was an ol' witch."

Dad sighed and rolled his eyes. Mom chuckled. I reached over and made Denny stick his spoon back into his bowl. There's nothing worse than gooey old oatmeal on the ceiling.

PUTNAM ♭BERKLEY

————————————online

**Your Internet gateway to a
virtual environment with
hundreds of entertaining and
enlightening books from
The Putnam Berkley Group.**

**While you're there visit the
PB Café and order-up the
latest buzz on the best
authors and books around—
Tom Clancy, Patricia Cornwell,
W.E.B. Griffin, Nora Roberts,
William Gibson, Robin Cook,
Brian Jacques, Jan Brett,
Catherine Coulter and
many more!**

**Putnam Berkley Online is located at
http://www.putnam.com**